Stella Díaz

Leaps to the Future

Also by Angela Dominguez

Stella Díaz Has Something to Say

Stella Díaz Never Gives Up

Stella Díaz Dreams Big

Stella Díaz to the Rescue

¡Ahí voy!

STELLA DÍAZ leaps TO THE FUTURE

ANGELA DOMINGUEZ

Roaring Brook Press
New York

Published by Roaring Brook Press
Roaring Brook Press is a division of Holtzbrinck Publishing
Holdings Limited Partnership
120 Broadway, New York, NY 10271 · mackids.com

Our books may be purchased in bulk for promotional, educational, or
business use. Please contact your local bookseller or the Macmillan Corporate
and Premium Sales Department at (800) 221-7945 ext. 5442 or by email at
MacmillanSpecialMarkets@macmillan.com.

Library of Congress Cataloging-in-Publication Data

Names: Dominguez, Angela, author.
Title: Stella Díaz leaps to the future / Angela Dominguez.
Description: First edition. | New York : Roaring Brook Press, 2023. |
   Series: Stella Díaz ; 5 | Audience: Ages 6–9. | Audience: Grades 2–3. |
   Summary: When fifth-grader Stella Díaz considers going to a different
   school than her closest friends, sees her big brother Nick receiving
   mail from colleges far away, and is forced to work on a project with her
   former bully, she suddenly realizes growing up is not quite as fun as
   she first thought.
Identifiers: LCCN 2022029744 | ISBN 9781250862570 (hardcover)
Subjects: CYAC: Friendship—Fiction. | Schools—Fiction. | Mexican
   Americans—Fiction.
Classification: LCC PZ7.D7114 Stl 2023 | DDC [Fic]—dc23
LC record available at https://lccn.loc.gov/2022029744

First edition, 2023
Book design by Veronica Mang
Printed in the United States of America by Lakeside Book Company,
Harrisonburg, Virginia

ISBN 978-1-250-86257-0 (hardcover)
1 3 5 7 9 10 8 6 4 2

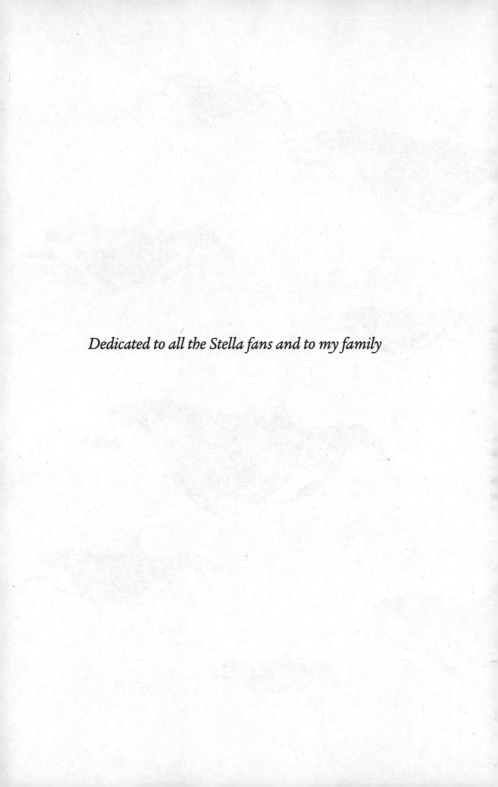

Dedicated to all the Stella fans and to my family

Chapter One

"What should I wear tomorrow?" I ask myself, standing in front of my closet. It's a huge decision because I'm about to start fifth grade!

I shuffle through my closet and drawers. My hand reaches out to a dress to examine it. Polka dots are my favorite, but is that what I should wear for the first day?

I put my hands on my hips. Maybe I should ask Stanley what he is going to wear since he's in my class this year. I know we're going to have so much fun working together like we did on the egg-drop project in fourth grade. I wonder what amazing new things we'll do together!

My head is filled with too many ideas, so I give up

looking for clothes. I decide to grab my notebook and review all my big plans for the new year. I've already jotted many ideas for the Sea Musketeers, like multiple fundraisers and matching T-shirts. As soon as I bend over to pick it up, my dog, Ramona, intercepts and licks my face. Then she softly growls, letting me know she's ready to play.

"Okay, girl," I say, clapping my hands together. "Let's go!"

I grab her squeaky dinosaur toy and toss it across my room. The stuffed toys with the crinkly paper inside are her favorites. Ramona always insists on playtime, which is more than okay with me.

I'm tugging with Ramona, who is fiercely holding the toy in her mouth, when I hear the door open. It's my brother, Nick, and he's holding Mom's phone.

"Hey, Stella," he whispers, "it's Dad. He wants to say hi."

I grab the phone from Nick. Dad usually calls twice a month on Sundays, but he's been on vacation in Mexico for a whole month. We weren't expecting to hear from him for a while.

I awkwardly say, "Hi . . . Dad. How's Mexico?"

"*¡Hola, mi amor! México está increíble.* I've been riding my bike and eating great food. You'd love it."

I sigh. That does sound incredible. Mom hardly ever goes on vacation, and when she does, it's for a few days or a week. Never a whole month. But I guess that is possible when you only have to worry about taking care of yourself.

He continues, "But enough about me, I wanted to wish you *buena suerte con el nuevo año de escuela.*"

"Really? Thanks, Dad!" I'm surprised he remembered that school is starting soon.

"*De nada.* You're getting so big. *Mi princesa* is in fourth grade!"

I feel my ears turn *roja* with frustration. There is a *huge* difference between fourth and fifth grade. The biggest is that it's my last year before middle school and

I'm no longer a baby. Instead of getting mad, though, I just correct him.

"It must be all the sun." He chuckles. "Of course, fifth grade."

We talk for a couple of minutes more and then we say our goodbyes. That's a typical phone call from my dad. He's like a little ghost crab. They are fun-looking crustaceans but hard to spot and disappear quickly. Sometimes they say something that pinches at your feelings, too. However, at least he called. He doesn't always remember the start of the school year.

Thankfully, my thoughts are interrupted by a soft scratching noise. Ramona is pawing at the door.

"C'mon, we better take you outside," I say, standing up.

I've barely opened the door when Ramona darts out of my room and down the stairs. Before I leave, I walk over to Pancho, my betta fish.

"We'll be back. You stay put, please."

He waves his fins in agreement. I giggle. That Pancho is one well-behaved fish.

Chapter Two

Mom is knitting on the couch when I come downstairs. I put her phone down on the coffee table, and she greets me with open arms.

"*Hola, mi niñita.*"

She can always sense when I need a hug. This, along with her amazing *albóndigas*, my favorite dinner, is why Mom is the best parent anyone could want.

"*¿Qué necesitas?*" she adds, asking what I need.

"Ramona needs to go on a walk, I think."

"Say nothing more." Mom rises from the couch and searches for her shoes.

Meanwhile, I find Ramona's leash and harness. Ramona is only twelve pounds, so it's easy to clip her in.

We found her on a dog-rescue site and adopted her on my tenth birthday. We're not exactly sure what kind of dog Ramona is. She looks like a chihuahua, but shaggier and bigger. Nick likes to call her baby Chewbacca. All I know is, she is super sweet and loves to cuddle.

I spy Nick sitting at the kitchen table. He's reading his PSAT workbook. That's a big test you take when you're in tenth grade before you take an even bigger test in eleventh grade. The *p* stands for "pre," but I'm not sure what *SAT* stands for. All I know is that it sounds like it will be a lot of work.

"Do you want to go on a walk with us?" I ask Nick. Ramona walks over to him like she's inviting him, too.

He gently pets her head. "No, I have my first study group this week. I should try reading this more."

I wink. "You mean *text* more."

Nick pushes away his phone and sticks out his tongue at me. He takes frequent breaks to check his phone for texts from Erika, his first official girlfriend. Then he looks back at his thick study guide. By the size of that book, I can tell he really does have a lot of reading to do.

Seeing Nick studying makes me wonder if I should prepare more for Mrs. Chen's class tomorrow. Mrs. Chen is going to be my fifth-grade teacher. I've never met her before, but I've seen her in the hallways at Arlington Heights Elementary. From what I can tell, she seems more serious than my previous teachers. That's probably because she teaches fifth grade and not one of the little-kid grades. At least I hope so.

Thankfully, Mom reappears ready for a walk and says, "Should we ask Linda if she wants to join?"

Linda is our next-door neighbor and a close family friend. I clap my hands together. "Yes! Maybe she can join us for dinner, too?"

A few minutes later, the five of us stand outside Linda's place. It's five if you include Ramona and her dog, Biscuit. As she locks her front door, Linda says wistfully, "I'm going to miss these impromptu walks."

Linda recently decided to move to an apartment. Somewhere where she doesn't have to worry about shoveling snow or climbing stairs. Thankfully, she's only

looking at places close by. Mom says I should be able to walk there with Ramona when I'm a little older, too.

Mom gives Linda a side hug.

"We will visit you all the time. Remember, you're welcome at our place whenever."

I pull Mom's shirt and wiggle my eyebrows at her.

"Oh, and please join us for dinner, too," Mom adds.

I grin, satisfied that she understood me.

Linda replies, "I'd love to join you all, but I have dinner plans with my family. They're helping me with the apartment search. Next time, I promise."

The five of us walk down the street side by side. For a second, I wonder how many more of these walks we will have until Linda moves. Linda is someone I can really talk to, and she can sense when something is on my mind. She won't be as easy to reach when she lives farther away. That thought pops out of my mind almost immediately because I feel a giant yank in my right arm. It's Ramona trying to chase a squirrel.

Now, as I try to pull Ramona back, my only thought is that she needs to take some behavior lessons from

Pancho. Luckily, Biscuit pounces at Ramona, inviting her to play with him instead of the squirrel. She agrees, and they begin to wag their tails at warp speed. I squeal with delight. Seeing the two of them gently paw at each other is one of the cutest things I've ever seen. Even cuter than a puffer fish.

Chapter Three

The next morning, I'm filled with excite-ment as we leave for school. I'm dressed in a shirt with tiny polka dots, which looks fun and slightly more grown up for my first day as a fifth grader. At least I think so. I'm sure Mrs. Chen will appreciate how mature I look.

"Bye, Ramona," I say as I scratch her ears. I double-check her water bowl before we head out.

It's hard leaving Ramona alone at home, but I love that she waits excitedly by the door when we return. Before Ramona, I had been wanting a dog of my own for years. That's why it feels amazing to see her so happy to greet me, because I feel the exact same way inside. Except I don't slobber all over her. Plus, Ramona has someone who walks her once a day, so she isn't by herself the whole time.

On the ride to school, I wish that Nick could drive me, because he looks like a cool older kid and not like a parent. However, high school starts before elementary, so that's impossible. I do like having a fun beat to shimmy along to with Mom. Salsa music matches my enthusiasm for the new school year. When Mom drops me off in front, she says, *"Que tengas un buen día en escuela."*

To which I reply, "Have a great day at work."

I walk toward the building with a strut. From the outside, I may look as cool as a sea cucumber, but on the inside, I'm as eager as Ramona at mealtime. I've been waiting for this. I just know school will be way easier now that I'm one of the oldest and tallest kids. I've also had five years of experience if you include kindergarten. This makes me a bona fide expert at Arlington Heights Elementary.

"Hi, Stella!" says my best friend, Jenny, running toward me.

I begin to say, "What did you do yesterday..." when I notice someone much shorter than me standing directly by my side. I look over. She has glasses and a short haircut, and, by the look on her face, she appears ready to burst with excitement.

"Umm, do you need something?" I ask.

"WOW." She beams from ear to ear. "You're Stella Díaz, right?"

I raise my eyebrows. "Yes...?"

She squeals. "I'm Gabby Torres! I'm in third grade, and I want to be a Sea Musketeer one day, just like you."

Gabby points over to a few friends of hers. They wave excitedly together.

"We're all fans," Gabby adds.

The Sea Musketeers is an organization I started with my friends the summer before fourth grade. Our mission is to protect the oceans and lower plastic consumption. We do fundraisers and wrote our own pledge to reduce ocean plastic. Last spring, we presented to the city council. It was scary to present in front of serious-looking grown-ups, but amazingly, they agreed to have our school district commit to the pledge and cut plastic use by 50 percent. Afterward, there was even an article in our local newspaper. Mom had it framed because it's *"muy especial."*

Jenny grins at me. I can tell she's amused. She's a Sea Musketeer, too.

Gabby continues, "And I'm already learning everything I can about the oceans and how I can protect them." She opens her backpack, pulls out a little journal, and starts reading.

"Like, did you know the ocean gives Earth an oxygen-rich atmosphere to make it possible for land animals to live?! Isn't that amazing?"

I shrug knowingly. "That's why the oceans are so important."

Gabby leans forward. "I knew you would."

Jenny looks at her watch and gasps. "Stella, we really need to get to our classes."

The corners of Gabby's mouth turn downward a little. "Oh . . . okay."

But then as quick as an on-off switch, she enthusiastically waves. "Nice to meet you Stella and Stella's friend! Next time I want to find out how I can join the Sea Musketeers."

We hear Gabby and her friends say goodbye in unison as Jenny and I walk away. I'm *roja* at first. I'm not used to having that much attention on me, but it quickly fades away. I mostly feel on top of the world. When I was in third grade, I was too shy to talk to anyone except for my family and Jenny. I was surprised if anyone knew my name. Now in fifth grade, I still can be occasionally a little shy, but I'm also apparently a celebrity. At least to Gabby and a small group of third graders.

I walk Jenny to her class and then walk across the hallway to mine. I remember how awful it was in third grade when we were in different classes. But now, it doesn't feel as bad. Plus, we still can eat lunch together.

The bell rings as I take my seat beside Stanley in the front row. I'm glad I have at least one best friend in my class!

I sit up very tall as Mrs. Chen calls attendance. When she does, I smile extra hard and project my voice loudly. After she reviews the classroom policies, I'm sitting on the edge of my seat, waiting for what's next. Then Mrs. Chen stands up.

"Let's not waste any time and begin our very first project. You'll be working in pairs."

I glance over at Stanley. He gently elbows me.

"Partners?" he whispers.

I give him a thumbs-up.

But to my surprise, Mrs. Chen starts assigning individual numbers. Oh no, this means we will be working in random groups! Random groups can be scary because you never know who you'll be paired up with. My heart races as she walks around the room saying "One, two, three . . . four" and so forth. I really hope I get to work with someone I like. She gives me the number three, and I hold my breath until I see my friend Isabel has the same number. Whew!

Mrs. Chen raises her arms. "Okay, find your partner."

As I walk over to Isabel, I frown when I see Jessica Anderson. She used to bully me in our third-grade class. Back then, she called me "Stella Stares" because I was afraid to speak out loud and would look wide-eyed when I was trying to get my words out. Thankfully, Mom taught me how to ignore her. It became especially easy in fourth grade, when we had different classes. However, it might not be the same now that she's in Mrs. Chen's class with me this year.

When I sit down next to Isabel, I look over to see who Stanley is paired with. My mouth drops as wide as a bigmouth fish. I can't believe it. It's Jessica Anderson! *Poor Stanley*, I think to myself, because

Jessica may be mean to Stanley because he's one of my closest friends. Stanley also knows how much she used to pick on me, so it might be hard for him to talk to her. At least I think he does. But then something even more surprising happens. Jessica and Stanley are both . . . smiling.

Chapter Four

"I'm so glad we're working together!"
Isabel says. "Did you have a good summer?"

"Uh-huh," I reply, mumbling. Like prey mesmerized by a glowing cuttlefish, I can't help but stare at Jessica and Stanley. I wish I were sitting closer to listen. It looks like they've stopped smiling. I think. Maybe Stanley smiled to be polite. He is a Texas gentleman, after all. I bet he's having a terrible time.

Mrs. Chen interrupts my thoughts. "Now that you've gotten to know your partner, I can explain the first part of the project."

She assigns each group one big problem caused by climate change. Our first task is to research the

problem and find the causes. At least, I think that is what she said. I keep glancing over at Jessica and Stanley from behind my notebook.

Isabel reads the assignment handout. "It looks like we're focusing on rising sea levels for our project. Do you have any ideas where to start, Stella? You're kind of an expert."

I whip back to Isabel. I feel embarrassed for being a bad partner. I shake it off and say, "Sorry. I was distracted. What about rising, ummm . . . levels?"

Isabel tilts her head. She seems confused. "Rising sea levels. It's our topic . . . Stella."

"Right. I thought you said something else," I reply with a nervous smile.

Isabel looks at me suspiciously for a second and heads to the computer station. We search online for facts on rising sea levels. I purposely choose a computer not too far from Stanley in case he needs my help with Jessica, although as soon as I start reading, I get hooked by the facts.

I point at the screen in disbelief. "Wow, the oceans have been rising since 1880, and most of it has been in the past twenty-five years."

Isabel adds with a frown, "That's because every year the average temperature keeps increasing, and it's melting glaciers."

I twirl one of my curls. It always helps me think. "There has to be something we can do."

We start searching for causes. Carbon dioxide emissions, like the ones from burning fossil fuels, are very much to blame. They get trapped in the atmosphere, and every bit of carbon is like another blanket on the planet and increases the temperature. But we discover a great, simple way to help combat it. If people plant more trees, then those would breathe in more carbon and there'd be less in the air. Trees are the world's natural and most effective air purifier. The more trees the better, say the experts. There is even a Plant a Billion Trees campaign by the Nature Conservancy. That sounds like an unbelievable number, but when you think of how big Earth is, that's completely possible.

After a while, Mrs. Chen announces to the class that it is lunchtime. I quickly catch up with Stanley at our usual lunch table in the cafeteria. His face is expressionless as he opens his Milky Way lunch box.

"So . . . how was it working with Jessica?" I ask, trying to sound calm. I hide my curious expression by opening my lunch box. I find my usual sunflower butter sandwich and carrot sticks. Mom did sneak in a treat. One single Gloria. It's the most spectacular Mexican candy. It has pecans and sweet caramel.

"It was fine," Stanley replies while munching on an

apple. He puts his hand on his chin. "Jessica actually has some great ideas if we have to do a presentation."

"Oh . . . really?" I reply, snapping a carrot stick with my hand in anger. I immediately feel embarrassed. I'm not sure what I was expecting, but it definitely wasn't Stanley complimenting Jessica.

Thankfully, Jenny arrives. "What are you guys talking about?" Jenny says as she sits down. She sometimes gets the school lunch, especially when it's chicken nuggets day like today. She dunks a nugget into ketchup and takes her signature small bite. She used to see how many bites she could get in a single piece of food. Her best record was ninety-seven in a single, tiny pretzel. She no longer does that, but she still takes awfully small bites.

Stanley folds his arms on the table. "Stella just asked me how it was to work with Jessica Anderson on a class project."

Jenny starts coughing and takes a sip of her water.

"Excuse me?" she replies. Jenny looks over at me, and I nod knowingly.

Stanley laughs. "I know that Jessica was mean to Stella in third grade—" then he shrugs "—but we're in fifth grade. People change."

"I don't think that's scientifically proven," I reply.

I take a hard bite of my sandwich, but as I chew, my mouth relaxes. I have a big realization. I am different now than I was in third grade. At least in some ways. I'm less shy, I own a dog, I have a whole group of friends, and I'm an American citizen, just to name a few things. But then I think about my dad. He's always been the same way, at least since I've known him. He's an example of someone who doesn't change. Maybe some people do change, but how can you tell?

"Just give her a chance," Stanley says. "For me."

Jenny and I look at each other and reluctantly reply, "Okay."

Then I glance over at Jessica Anderson across the cafeteria. I know I've changed. But the big question is: Has Jessica Anderson changed? Or is she still a bully in disguise?

Chapter Five

By the next Monday, I'm relieved to be
going to art club. The first week at school has been
fine, but my new class has been harder, and we've had
homework almost every night. Worse, it's been strange
sharing Stanley with Jessica in class. Turns out our
group assignment is a big project, and we'll be working with our partners once a week for a few weeks.
Researching our topic has been upsetting, too. I guess
some changes can be good, but other ones, like rising
sea levels, are not good at all. That's why, as soon as I
see Ms. Benedetto, I run and give her a hug.

"Stella, how is fifth grade?" she asks, giving me a
hug back.

"Good . . ." I sigh. "Just different."

Ms. Benedetto was my fourth-grade teacher and is probably my favorite teacher I've ever had. She is way different from Mrs. Chen, who rarely chats with me before class. I've tried, but she says she needs quiet time to prepare. I guess that makes sense. I hope it's not because she doesn't like me. All I know is, I miss sharing my artwork or an ocean fact every morning with my teacher. For instance, I discovered that every whale shark has a unique set of spots like a human fingerprint. I've been wanting to share that all day. But before I can say my fun fact, Ms. Benedetto says, "Hold on one second."

She walks over to her bag and pulls out a pamphlet, handing it to me.

"I have something that may brighten your day."

The pamphlet feels like fancy, thick stationery, not like flimsy notebook paper. In big, bold letters, it says CHICAGO ART AND SCIENCE MAGNET SCHOOL.

"What's this?" I ask.

Ms. Benedetto clasps her hands excitedly. "It's a magnet middle school for students interested in science and the arts. Since this is your last year at Arlington Heights, I immediately thought of you."

I point at myself. "Me?"

I carefully open the fancy pamphlet and add, "But isn't it expensive?"

She shakes her head. "They have an endowment. That basically means the tuition is free."

My eyes grow large before I can say anything. Ms. Benedetto continues, "However, there is a tough application process, and only a few kids get in every year."

I gulp. That sounds intimidating. It feels as rare as seeing a vampire squid in real life. While they are real animals, they live far below in the midnight zones of the tropical and temperate oceans. It's a place where no light can reach, so it's super dark. It's also so far down that it's dangerous for people to visit. Although I hope to see it one day.

She puts her hands on my shoulders. "I've sent an email to your mom, but I want you to take this pamphlet and check it out. Talk it over with her, but in my opinion, this school was built for a kid like you."

As I begin looking through the pamphlet, my worried face breaks into a grin. I feel all the hairs on my arms stand up. This looks like an amazing school that's perfect for my top two interests. Best of all, Ms. Benedetto thinks I'm special enough to go.

I bounce a little with excitement and reply, "Okay."

I'm about to thank Ms. Benedetto when Mr. Foster, the art teacher, walks over.

He asks, "Almost ready to start the meeting?"

She nods and motions me to sit down. Mr. Foster runs the club with Ms. Benedetto. They are also engaged and plan to get married during the winter break.

Over at my table, I stare at the pamphlet. There are pictures of kids painting, sculpting, and working with robots. Could I really be one of these smiling kids in the pictures?

Suddenly, I hear a loud, excited voice across the room. "Wait! WOW! You love art, too?"

I recognize that voice from the first day. It's Gabby, and she is diving right toward me. I quickly put the pamphlet under my sketchbook and then sort of awkwardly smile.

Gabby waves and sits down in the empty chair beside me. It's the seat that Anna used to sit in, but her family moved over the summer to Wisconsin. I was a little sad that Anna left, but we've been sending letters back and forth with drawings.

When I glance over at Gabby, her cheeks look like a kettle about to boil over with joy. My friend Chris is in the third chair at our table. He has become one of my newest and closest friends ever since we both joined art club. We grew especially close last year after I made a bunch of mistakes when I found out his dad has primary lateral sclerosis and needs to be in a wheelchair. I've learned to be more understanding and, most importantly, focus on all the things Mr. Pollard is able to do instead of his disability.

"Hi! I'm Chris." He waves to Gabby.

She introduces herself and then wiggles around

to face me. "I'm so excited for art club. I've thought about it all day. It's like a song you can't get out of your head." Gabby turns a little *roja*. "Sorry, I ramble when I'm nervous."

I softly chuckle to myself. That's the opposite problem I have when I am nervous! I just clam up.

"I'm excited, too," Chris says with an understanding expression.

Ms. Benedetto calls Chris up to the front, and I see her give him a pamphlet to the magnet school as well. Chris is the best artist at the school, not to mention his parents are big art fans. They even have a van with the license plate VAN GO. He'd be a perfect fit for the school. I hope he applies.

Meanwhile, Gabby empties her backpack on the table in front of me. I notice the journal I saw earlier, but I also spot a dog-eared sketchbook. Gabby flips it open, and I spy drawings of sea creatures and animals all inside. I'm surprised. It looks like one of my sketchbooks. Although mine is now filled with many drawings of Ramona besides all the marine animals. I guess

Gabby and I do share a few things in common. I point at her sketch of a seahorse.

"This is great!"

She squeals. "Really? Thank you!"

I lean over to share one of my favorite facts. "Did you know that seahorses swim vertically and sea dragons swim horizontally?"

She shakes her head. "That's so cool."

I grin. "I think so, too."

When Nick and I get back home from school and after we walk Ramona, I sit down at my desk. Instead of working on homework, though, I grab my sketchbook. I draw all the activities I could do at my "maybe future" middle school. I'm so absorbed in my drawings that I don't hear Mom come home. I'm surprised when she gives me a kiss on the head.

"What are you drawing?" She studies my drawing for clues.

I turn *roja*. "Ms. Benedetto told me about a special middle school I could attend. I want to apply!"

I run over to my backpack and hand her the pamphlet to the magnet school. At first, Mom is silent as she studies it. Then I see a smile. "It does look like an interesting school," Mom says. "Would you like to take a peek at their website?"

"Yes!" I jump out of my chair and follow her to the laptop.

The website is way fancier than the pamphlet. It starts with a video that looks like a movie with inspirational music, the sort of music they play during the Olympics. All the students seem so happy, too. As I sit there, I imagine myself standing among them.

"Mom, I want to go!" I say, throwing my arms in the air. "Oh, I wish I could skip fifth grade and just go there tomorrow!" Then I slump over dramatically.

Mom puts her arm around my shoulder.

"*Niñita*, this school is very exciting, but you're in fifth grade right now. It's a special time, too. You only get to do this once. *Disfrútala*."

I force myself to agree. Mom is always telling me to slow down, enjoy things, and not to worry about growing up. In her words, "You only have a few years to be a kid, and life naturally gets more complicated as you get older." I kind of understand what she means, but I also think they didn't have schools like this when she was my age. This is probably why she doesn't understand how exciting it is.

Mom tugs at my sleeve. "*Vámonos*, let's go check on the other big kid in this house and eat some dinner."

"Do you mean Ramona? She's right here on my lap." Ramona is curled up and snoring. For such a small dog, she can be awfully loud.

"*Qué chistosa*," Mom replies. "C'mon. You know I mean *el niño*. He needs a break."

That's true. Nick has been studying in his room since we got home from school. Then I pick up Ramona and reluctantly walk away from the laptop with Mom.

Chapter Six

I love breakfast on Saturdays. Some-times we get donuts, and sometimes Mom surprises us with a super delicious breakfast. This morning she made *chilaquiles*. It sounds like it might be spicy because of the "chila" part, but it's just tortillas baked with salsa and yummy, crumbly cheese.

It's because on Saturdays, we all need extra fuel. Nick is usually working at the pizza shop, and now that his foot is completely healed, he's back to karate class, too. I'm just as busy because I have my weekly Sea Musketeers meeting on Saturdays. All that extra talking makes me hungry.

Before we begin our busy day, Mom shows Nick

and me an email about the magnet school application from my school counselor, Mr. Barkley. Mom emailed him as soon as we decided to apply.

"Stella," Mom says, "it looks like there are three parts to your application."

I gulp. *Ay caramba*, that sounds like a lot.

Nick elbows me. "That's not too bad, and it looks like it's due in March." He leans back. "See? You've got plenty of time."

"Really?" I reply, inching closer to the screen.

He's right. March 15 is the official due date. That's six whole months away. It's plenty of time. However, I gulp again when I read that Mr. Barkley mentions that very few students get in. That's what Ms. Benedetto said, too!

I move back in my seat. I'll let Mom read this aloud to me. It will sound less intimidating if she says it.

"What are the three parts, Mom?" I ask, pushing my fork around on my plate.

"*Número uno*, you're going to need to record a video on 'what are your biggest accomplishments.'"

My stomach starts to feel funny. I hate being on video. I usually run and hide. There is something about the combination of my voice and seeing my own face in action that *no me gusta*. However, if Mom and Nick help me, it could be easier.

Mom continues, *"Número dos*, you'll also write an essay, Stella. It's on 'who you admire the most and why.'"

That is exciting and super easy, I think to myself. I love writing, and I also have so many idols, from Jacques Cousteau to Vincent van Gogh. Choosing one will be the difficult part.

"*Número tres*, you'll have to create an original piece of art."

I clasp my hands together. Now that will be a piece of cake! The hardest part will be deciding what to draw.

"And that's it!" Mom says as she stands up.

"Does he say anything else?" I am sitting on the edge of my seat.

"Just that he'll work on writing you a letter of recommendation, your transcript . . ." Mom shrugs.

"And that *mi Stellita* is a real go-getter with an excellent chance to get in."

"Me?" I squeal. It feels like my dream may come true.

"Of course she does," says Nick, messing with my curls.

Mom looks me in my eyes. "*¿Qué piensas*, Stella? It's a lot of work. Are you sure you still want to apply?"

I stretch my arms out wide. "Absolutely! I want to get started today!"

I tug at Nick. "Can you help me brainstorm?"

My mind is so overflowing with thoughts that I begin to ramble. "I mean, do I write about van Gogh or Cousteau? And what are my accomplishments? What even makes a good accomplishment, Nick?"

Nick grins at first, but then he looks at his watch. "Sorry, kiddo, not right now. I've got to get ready for work and karate!"

I frown a little. Nick is busier than ever. I know school gets harder each year, so I sort of expected it, but not as much as this. Now that he has a girlfriend and the PSATs to worry about, I see him even less.

But luckily, I am not sad for long, because Mom says, "And you have to get ready for your club, Stella."

I stand up. "Yikes! You're right."

I immediately run upstairs. We are holding the Sea Musketeers meeting at my house today. Part of the agreement with Mom is that I must clean my room before the group shows up. I just barely finish when Mariel arrives. Mariel used to come early to tutor me in Spanish. Since then, she always shows up first.

"¡*Hola*, Stella!"

"¡*Buenas tardes*, Mariel!" I reply.

As we set up the sitting arrangement for the club meeting in my room, she notices the pamphlet for the magnet school on my desk.

"Wait, are you applying to Chicago Art and Science?"

I turn around. "I am!"

"Me too!" Mariel starts jumping up and down. "Can you imagine if we both get in?"

I join her in a jumping fiesta. It would be so fun to be in the same school next year!

Nick walks by in his karate uniform with car keys in hand, watching us as we hop and scream. "Girls," he groans, but he follows it up with a wink.

Eventually we calm down. Then I realize something. "Don't say anything to the group, though. It might jinx us if we tell them, and then we won't get in."

"Or . . . ," Mariel says, staring at the ground, "it would be super embarrassing if only one of us is accepted."

Oh no, Mariel is right. And wait, this means I'm technically in competition with her for a spot at the school! While it would be sad if she didn't get in, I think I might be more upset if Mariel is accepted over me. I wonder if she's thinking the same thing.

Mariel breaks the silence. "I hate that the school takes only a few students."

"We'll just have to help each other to get in," I say, pretending to be confident.

"*¡Claro que sí!*" replies Mariel.

Then we both cross our fingers on both hands in solidarity.

When the rest of the group shows up, we stop all discussion about the magnet school, as promised. The club meeting starts after I call attendance and check everyone off. It's my job as copresident. Then Logan, our other copresident, reviews our agenda.

Logan reads off the list. "Priority number one. We need to plan our fall fundraiser."

Stanley grabs the toy orca to speak. "I have an idea."

Everyone leans in excitedly.

Stanley continues, "Stella and I are learning about climate change in our class. And I think we should focus on that."

I grab the orca from Stanley. "I love it! There is a campaign called Plant a Billion Trees to help combat carbon emissions. Maybe we could plant trees at our next event?"

Logan scratches his chin. "That's a great idea, but we probably should do something ocean-related, too. We're the Sea Musketeers, after all."

"Well, clean air means healthy oceans," I reply.

Jenny nods. "That's true!"

Stanley adds, "I have an idea that might do that. My dad told me all about this Billion Oyster Project. In New

York, this organization is filling the waterways with oysters and restoring their populations. Oysters are like the natural filters of the sea. They purify the water so that the rest of the marine animals can thrive better."

Kristen sits up. "Oh! It can be a 'Plant a Tree and Save an Oyster' event, or better yet, 'Billions of Oysters and Trees' event!" Her eyes go wide, and she covers her mouth. Only the person holding the toy orca should be speaking, but we often forget.

I glance at Stanley, who hands me the toy orca, and I reply, "I think that's a great idea, Kristen!"

Logan smiles. I'm happy he agrees. "Raise your hand if you agree this should be our next fundraiser," I say.

We all raise our hands, including Logan, although

he likes to wait for the last moment. He can be a little dramatic.

"Great!" Mariel says. "We should start planning it soon. Let's put the event on the calendar."

I pull out the calendar and lay it in front of the group. I wonder if this is a good time to mention the idea of doing a couple of fundraisers this fall.

Before I can suggest it, Kristen says, "I won't be able to do any planning next week. I am finally getting my braces off on Saturday."

She flashes her shiny mouth and points at her teeth with excitement.

Jenny chimes in. "Yeah, I have a dance competition that weekend, too." That's not surprising. Jenny sometimes skips Sea Musketeers meetings for her dance studio, but she attends most meetings.

Stanley looks embarrassed when he says, "I have to skip it, too. We have a family get-together."

One by one, everyone but me can't attend next week. Then we realize that for the very first time, we have to cancel our regular weekly meeting.

"I can't believe it," I say, staring around the room.

Logan shakes his head. "Don't worry about it. It's one time in over a year. That's like one in over fifty meetings. No big deal."

But that's not true, I think to myself. Kristen is already in middle school, and next year will be the first year for the rest of us. We're all going to get even busier. I've seen it with my own brother. Will we eventually become too busy for the Sea Musketeers? Will the club even exist for kids like Gabby?

Chapter Seven

While many things are different in fifth grade, I'm so happy there is still sustained reading time. It's a nice, quiet break from all the classwork. It's also a time I can do research for my application essay. Ms. Morales, my school librarian, helps me find a stellar stack of books on people I admire. I'm starting with Frida Kahlo since she's a woman who accomplished many things as an artist. As I read my book, I discover she had plans to attend medical school before she became a famous artist. It's awesome that she loved both art and science. It's just like me. I'm eager to find out more, but the timer rings and Mrs. Chen resumes class.

"Next on the agenda, I have a very exciting fifth-grade project I want to share with you all."

Gasp! Could it be another mural? We painted one in the library as part of an art club activity. It's filled with dolphins, our school's mascot. I was going to include it as one of my accomplishments for the video, but I'd love to do another one and maybe it could be part of my art project for the magnet school. Ms. Benedetto said I should do a few art projects, and she would help me pick one to include with my application.

"Oh, is it a talent show?" Ben asks. "I've been practicing my drums."

I giggle. Ben loves to make a lot of noise. It's only fitting that he would play the drums, too.

She raises her fingers to remind the class to be quiet. "We're doing a time capsule. Since the school is celebrating its fiftieth year, we thought it would be a great idea to recognize it with something special. Each fifth-grade class will contribute one item to the capsule."

I clasp my hands together. It's something I've only read about in books, and now we're doing one in real life at school.

Stanley raises his hand. Mrs. Chen calls on him.

"Is it going to be like the Golden Record that NASA sent into outer space on Voyager? It has images and all these records from planet Earth."

I look over at Stanley with amazement. He knows just as much about outer space as I do about the oceans. He's certainly taught me a lot. I'm going to miss that if we end up going to different schools.

Mrs. Chen responds, "Great observation, Stanley. Ours will be less high tech, but it's sort of the same idea. It will be a collection of items that fifth graders deem noteworthy. Things we'd like people to dig up many years from now."

I grab my face with my hands. This is just so exciting.

"And we're looking for a couple of volunteers to help choose and work on our class contribution. You'll get extra credit, too."

This might be a good detail to include in my application video. Making a time capsule does sound like it could be an accomplishment.

I raise my hand. I glance around the room, and to my surprise, Jessica Anderson has her hand up, too.

"Great. You two can be the class volunteers. Come see me before lunch and I'll tell you all the details."

I glance over at Jessica. She's sort of expressionless, but I swear I see a small smirk. I whip my head around to face forward. I suddenly feel nervous. I start to consider withdrawing from the project, but then I shake my head. Stanley says Jessica has changed, and I'm more confident than I used to be. I also haven't fallen in front of the whole class since third grade, so there shouldn't be anything she can make fun of.

The class works on math before lunch. When the bell rings, I walk over to Mrs. Chen's desk. When I make eye contact with Jessica, I bump my hip into a desk. I hear her giggle softly. I turn a little *roja* and try to walk confidently like it's no big deal.

Mrs. Chen types on the computer. "I'm going to send your parents a release form by email. If they agree, then you two will coordinate our class contribution. Any questions?"

"How often will we meet?" Jessica asks.

That's a good question, I think. Why didn't I ask that first?

Mrs. Chen looks at her calendar. "Once a month after school. I'll coordinate with your parents the best time to meet."

"Perfect," says Jessica.

"Yeah . . . ," I reply, loudly and awkwardly. I want to hide my face. I don't know why, after all these years, she still makes me a little nervous.

"Great!" Mrs. Chen responds, then dismisses us to lunch.

Jessica and I walk silently toward the cafeteria. I ball my fists together. *I can do this*, I think to myself. I've changed. I'm more confident, right? I take a deep breath and say, "I'm excited to work on the time capsule with you, uh . . . Jessica."

Jessica sort of shrugs. "Yeah, the project should be fun."

Then she walks away toward her regular lunch table.

That wasn't awful. It could have been worse. Maybe it won't be so bad. However, when I sit back at my table with Stanley and Jenny, I hear a loud laugh from Jessica's table. I turn around to look. It doesn't seem like they are laughing at me. But I'm not sure either. What have I signed myself up for?

Chapter Eight

During the school announcements, Mrs. Chen hands back our weekend homework. As we wait, Stanley sneaks me a piece of strawberry-flavored taffy. I try to chew without moving my mouth too much. We're not supposed to eat in class, but it's just one piece. Plus, it's mid-October, so there is more candy floating around for Halloween. It's hard not to have one! All I know is, I'm eager to see my grade. I wrote a personal narrative about the first time I saw the ocean. It was when we were in Mexico visiting my *tía* Maria. I used so many great adjectives. It's like I painted a picture with my words. When I receive my paper, I flip it over confidently. One look at my grade, though, and I almost spit out my candy.

This can't be true. To my horror, at the top of my paper, instead of my usual A with a star or smiley face, there is a C minus.

I, Stella Díaz, have received a bad grade.

I hide my paper under my notebook. Surely this must be a mistake. Maybe Mrs. Chen read someone else's paper and got confused. I've mislabeled things before. Like once, I mixed up sugar and salt when I was making chocolate chip cookies with Nick, and that was *no bueno*.

I wait until lunchtime to find out whether this grade is a mistake. Stanley tries to wait for me before he heads to the cafeteria, but I tell him I need to speak to Mrs. Chen first.

I take a deep breath and walk to her desk. She's

busy grabbing her purse and lunch bag. She looks up at me.

"Oh hi, Stella. Do you have a question?"

I bite my lip.

Mrs. Chen asks, "Is it about the time capsule? Don't worry, I received your signed permission slip. We'll meet in a couple of weeks."

I shake my head. It takes me a second to get the words out. I try not to, but my voice wobbles a little bit. "I'm wondering why I received a bad grade on the writing assignment. I've only ever received As before on my papers."

She motions me to sit down.

"Your story was great, but there are definitely some grammar issues. We're in fifth grade now, and we want to make sure you break out of some bad habits."

Then she reviews the paper with me. In some ways, I understand what she is saying, but I wonder why no one has ever pointed this out before. For instance, I keep flipping back and forth between the present and past tense in my story. Apparently, it can be confusing to the reader. I also switch the placement of the verbs and nouns sometimes. None of this has affected my grade before, but I guess in fifth grade, people expect you to have all the language issues figured out.

She leans in. "You know. I've struggled with grammar myself."

"Really?" I reply. I'm shocked. Everything about Mrs. Chen is tidy and organized. I've never seen a hair out of place, while my curls do whatever they please.

"For a non-native speaker, English grammar can be tricky. I should know. Mandarin was my first language."

"I didn't know that," I say. On the first day, she told us only a little bit about herself. She did mention she was Chinese American, but I assumed that because I didn't hear an accent, English was her first language.

She gives me a reassuring nod.

It's nice to hear that Mrs. Chen can relate to my experiences, but the situation is a little frustrating, too. I had to take three years of speech classes with Ms. Thompson to improve my pronunciation. Once

I graduated, I thought all my English struggles were behind me, but apparently, they aren't.

Mrs. Chen touches my arm. "It's okay to get a lower grade on an assignment, Stella, especially if you learn from it. You're still a stellar student. If you'd like to resubmit the essay with changes, I'd be happy to regrade it."

I feel a little bit better. This is also the nicest Mrs. Chen has been to me, but it's not like I like the circumstances. Or is it that I dislike them? Which one is better grammatically? I sigh, feeling confused about language as I walk toward the cafeteria. It's a bummer to realize that writing the application essay is going to be harder than I thought. At least I'll have Mom to proofread it, but still, maybe some of my bad grammar will slip through and I will lose my chance to get into the magnet school.

Thankfully, after lunch, we move on to science. This should make me feel better because this is sort of my area of expertise. At least I think so.

For our science lesson, we finally present our climate change project. Not only do we have to present the causes, but we also have to show solutions to our problem. Isabel and I go first. I feel great because our visuals are a real standout. Isabel also had the genius idea of handing out a seed to everyone in class to encourage them to plant a tree. They're sunflower seeds instead of real tree seeds, but I can tell Mrs. Chen was impressed by the gesture, because she gives us a thumbs-up.

Stanley and Jessica are the last to present. Their project is on the problems farming will face in the future. If the planet continues to warm up, farming will have to become even more sustainable in tougher conditions. Like, some places that get a lot of rain for farms might not anymore, and others might get too much. I never thought of that before. Anyway, I was half expecting Jessica to read from note cards like she did in third grade, but she has everything memorized. She even had a poem to encourage people to eat sustainably!

It's hard to admit it, but they are probably the best presentation of the day. At least tied with mine and Isabel's. Most surprising of all, they both look like they are having fun. Wait, does Stanley like Jessica more than me? I groan. Between school, my friendships, and the application, it's like competition is everywhere! I wish I could run home and cuddle with Ramona right now.

Later, when school ends, Stanley and I walk toward the main entrance together.

Stanley pats my backpack. "Stella, your presentation was amazing!"

I try to look happy, but my face turns into a strange frowny smile.

Stanley looks surprised. "Hey, what's wrong?"

I was hoping to keep my application a secret for a bit longer. I don't want to jinx myself, but the weight of the secret feels heavier than my backpack. I cave in and let it out.

"I'm feeling a little worried." I pause. "I'm applying to the Chicago Art and Science Magnet School for next school year. It's really hard to get in. I worry that I won't make the cut."

"Wow! That sounds awesome." Stanley crosses his arms and looks at me. "And no way will you not get in. You're the smartest kid I know!"

I grin, but as I start to think about it, I realize the most awful thing. Something as big as the ocean that

I hadn't considered until now. If I attend the magnet school, then I will be in a different school than Jenny, Stanley, and most of my other friends. This means I won't see them every day and share my lunch with them. When I work on exciting projects, it will be with strangers. I start feeling my stomach twist into knots. I glance over at Stanley.

He takes the words right out of my mouth. "It's going to be weird not having you in the same school."

I scrunch my face.

"But we'll see each other every week at the Sea Musketeers meeting."

"That's true," I reply, nodding. That makes me feel a little better.

He elbows me in the side. "Plus, who else am I going to ride bikes with? That's our hangout time."

He's right. I can imagine all the exciting things from school I'll have to talk about every time we hang out. I won't even need "conversation starters" anymore. That's what I call fun facts that I collect in my journal.

They can be useful whenever I'm struggling to talk with someone.

"Promise we'll always be friends?" I ask, pushing the front door open.

Stanley sticks out a pinkie, and we do possibly the strongest pinkie promise I've ever done.

Chapter Nine

My favorite days of the week are art club days. This year it feels like art club, more and more, is the best part of my day.

I sit down in my regular spot next to Gabby and Chris. We're working on collages today, using an assortment of magazines, paper, scissors, and glue. Ms. Benedetto suggests I brainstorm collage ideas for my original art piece for the magnet school application. I grab all the blue images I can find since it's my favorite color. All I know is, sometimes, nothing is more soothing than cutting paper.

I'm still a little quiet after my long day of school. Thankfully, Chris starts talking.

"Stella, I looked into the Chicago Art and Science school that Ms. Benedetto mentioned to us. I'm applying, too!"

My eyes light up. If Chris and Mariel both go, I will have two friends with me! I am about to lift my hand to give him a high five when I remember this means I'll be going against him for a spot to attend. More and more, I feel like I'm in a tournament to win against my own friends. It's as if we are those sea creatures at the Japanese aquarium that competed with each other during the Tokyo Olympics. Except we're not battling one another for medals, we are dueling it out for our future! And Chris is a really talented artist, too. Gulp, I'm going to have to try even harder.

Gabby pipes in. "That sounds so cool. Almost as cool as a flashlight fish. Did you know it has an organ under its eye that produces light?"

I smile back hesitantly. I love sharing sea creature facts, but now is not the time.

I'm more curious to see how far along Chris is with the application. With it due five months away, maybe he hasn't even thought about it.

"What are you doing for the video part?" I ask Chris as I stick a piece of paper down onto the board. I try to appear as casual as possible.

"I'm not sure yet," he replies.

I sigh with relief at first, but then he goes on. "But I know I want it to look interesting. My mom has friends who are game designers. They have a green screen, so I can put whatever background I like on the video. I'm thinking of using an art museum like the Art Institute."

I gulp. We were going to just use the video on my mom's phone! Mom and I will need to step up our game.

He continues, "And for the essay, I am thinking about writing about my dad. He's my hero."

"I'm sure he'd love that." That's such a great idea and very special to Chris.

Then I realize I really need to narrow down soon who I'll write about for my essay. We go back to cutting paper for our collages in silence. The sounds of snipping help to distract me from my application nerves. Suddenly, Gabby clears her throat.

"Umm . . . Stella?"

I glance over and raise an eyebrow.

She drops her scissors and puts both hands on the table. I can see the enthusiasm build.

"How do I become a Sea Musketeer? It's my biggest dream."

I pause and think. The club has never discussed adding new members. I guess we haven't had anyone ask before either. Still, I do think we have the perfect amount of people now. We used to have seven, which some say is lucky, but our group nowadays is six. It's a nice even number. But Gabby really does care about the oceans. I think about how Mom responds in these sorts of situations.

"Let me get back to you, Gabby. I'd have to talk to the rest of the club. I'm only the copresident after all."

"Oh . . . ," she replies. She hunches over and looks the smallest I've ever seen her.

I feel a little bad, so I lean over and say, "It's definitely maybe. I will check soon."

She starts to grin a little. "Thanks, Stella."

Chapter Ten

After I tell Mom and Nick about Chris's plans for his application and how it made me feel nervous, they recommend we try doing a practice video.

"This way, by the time we do the official recording," Mom says, "you'll feel natural in front of the camera."

"And just be yourself," Nick adds. "I mean, you're pretty cool, and I'm not saying that because I'm your big brother."

My heart feels like it may burst. It's amazing to have them helping.

Before we get started, Nick suggests I write my talking points on note cards. While Mom and Nick set up the recording station, I jot down some of my accomplishments. For instance, I mention the big projects I've done with my groups, like the Sea Musketeers and art club. I also list all the things I've done in school and, of course, the Shedd summer camp.

When I finish my notes, I feel ready. I definitely dislike being recorded, but I am so excited about the application. I'm even more excited than before because I had another big realization the other day. If I get into the magnet school, I may never have to see Jessica Anderson again in my entire life! I'll never have to be reminded about how awkward and shy I can be. In fact, I could have a clean slate. Everyone at my new school will think I am just naturally confident! I could even get a makeover to really start things fresh.

As I stand in front of the mirror in my room, I adjust my lucky outfit, one of my starfish shirts. Then I pause. Is this outfit magnet school material? I have a feeling it's not, so I quickly change into my navy striped sweater instead. This looks more academic, I think. Then I touch my hair and get an idea. I pull all my curls into a bun with a hair tie, then turn around and face Ramona.

"What do you think?"

She tilts her head at me with a confused expression.

"You're right." It feels strange and not like me, so I let my curls loose.

When I am ready, I walk downstairs to the living room, where Mom is setting up the tripod. Maybe Mom will have some good ideas about a new hairstyle. When I mention it to her, she looks surprised.

She walks over and touches my curls. "What do you mean change *tu pelo*?"

I shrug. "I don't know. Maybe I could straighten it. That's what sophisticated girls do."

Mom shakes her head. "*Mi Stellita*, you're too young for that."

"You're right." I stare at the mirror. "I also like my curls too much."

Mom studies my face closely and says, "What if you grow out your hair? Maybe try some new hair accessories?"

MAKEOVERS

I place my hand on my chin. I guess that could be sort of different and fun. I always wear a headband because it keeps the hair out of my face, but I could try something new when I start middle school. I could try a barrette. Maybe they sell ones with sea creatures, too!

Nick comes in with an extra lamp to brighten up the room. Then Mom places the camera on top of the tripod. They both double-check the camera to make sure it looks good, and Mom gives me a thumbs-up.

"Ready, sis?" Nick asks, standing behind the camera.

I give him a thumbs-up, and he presses RECORD. After he says, "Go," I begin reading from my note cards. I try not to look too much as I present. When I reach the phrase that I'm "academically successful," I stop dead in my tracks. All my ideas vanish, and I just turn *roja*. Saying it aloud, I realize I am not as academically successful, at least not anymore. Mrs. Chen gave me a higher grade for my personal narrative essay when I resubmitted it, but I've still been getting Bs on my writing. It's crickets until Nick says, "All right. Let's take two."

I quickly review my notes again. I take a deep breath. On the second try, I only manage to say, "My name is Stella Díaz" before stumbling over the words "Chicago Art and Science Magnet School." It's a tongue twister, especially when you're feeling nervous.

Mom and Nick look at each other.

"It's okay, Stella," Nick says. "This is just practice."

I throw my face into my hands. At this rate, it might take all night.

Nick quickly picks up Ramona, who is sitting on the floor. "Ramona thinks you're doing a great job. See?"

Then he puts her on my lap. Her slobbery licks on my face make me feel better, but it's the lick up my nose that makes me erupt with laughter.

"Eww, gross!" I reply between giggles.

Laughter must be contagious, because Mom and Nick start giggling, too. Before we know it, all our eyes are watering from laughing too much.

Mom says, wiping away tears, "Okay, I know what to do."

Mom grabs her phone and begins playing her favorite salsa song, "Vivir Mi Vida" by Marc Anthony. She then twirls me around like we're salsa dancing, and Nick joins for a second. He doesn't love dancing, but Mom can convince him for a minute.

"Let's give the video another shot," Nick says after our wiggle break.

The third attempt does the trick, because I'm able to speak through all my talking points without stopping or turning *roja*.

"How was that?" I ask.

Mom replies, "*¡Perfecto!*"

Nick gives me a high five. "Excellent practice. With the essay, you'll be golden."

I sigh contentedly. Once I say all my accomplishments aloud, I'm reminded that I have done many things over the past few years. The Sea Musketeers pledge, volunteering, painting a mural, a spelling bee, and the city council presentation, just to name a few. I've even improved my Spanish! Maybe I should just focus on myself and my application rather than comparing myself with Mariel and Chris. I think I'll be happier this way. All I know is, with everything changing and all the pressure of the application, it's nice that I have Nick and Mom to help me out. Better yet, to giggle with, too.

Chapter Eleven

When Mom drops me off at school in the morning, she wishes me good luck on the time capsule project. She doesn't know how much I need it. I never mentioned to her that I'd be working with Jessica Anderson. I was afraid she might tell me not to do it. She knows only about the extra credit part and that it might look good on the school application. I figure I'll have Mrs. Chen there. What is the worst that can happen, right?

However, as soon as I am alone for the first time with Jessica and Mrs. Chen, the butterflies take over my body. I stare at the cookie Stanley left me on his way out. Sharing M&M cookies is one of Stanley's ways to make new friends. I consider sharing it with Jessica, but the thought makes me too anxious. I nervously nibble on it as Mrs. Chen sits down across from us.

"Thank you, ladies, for volunteering to be a part of this special project."

I fidget while Jessica smiles politely.

"You two will oversee our class contribution. This time capsule won't be opened for twenty-five years, so it really needs to show a slice of life of your fifth-grade class and experience at Arlington Heights."

"Wow," I whisper.

"Have you two ever worked together before?" Mrs. Chen asks.

I shake my head. I open my mouth to explain more, but I close it. I don't know how to say nicely that Jessica can be a bully, which is why we never worked together before.

"We were in third grade together . . . ," Jessica replies. I notice a small smirk, or at least I think I see one.

I immediately cross my arms and stare at her. Then Jessica does the same.

Mrs. Chen looks at the two of us. You could cut the tension with a knife.

"Are you two going to be okay working together? We're spending quite a bit of time on this project, and I want to make sure it goes smoothly."

"Yes, we're fine," I reply.

Jessica nods.

Mrs. Chen looks at us. "Happy to hear that."

Mrs. Chen pulls out a flyer about the time capsule. We read it silently for a few minutes. As I read, the excitement for the project starts to take over, and my nerves begin to leave my body. My brain starts to come up with so many ideas.

"I want you to imagine yourselves as adults. It's twenty-five years in the future," Mrs. Chen continues. "What would you want to see? How do you want to feel?"

I try to imagine the future. I'll probably be as tall as Mom. Maybe as tall as Nick. Other than that, it's hard to picture it. Will there be robots and flying cars? From what I can tell in the movies, they have been saying that forever. Could that actually happen? Then I look over at Jessica. She looks as perplexed as I feel.

"Maybe it should be a movie?" I suggest hesitantly.

"Or something high tech. Since it's in the future?" Jessica chimes in.

"Great suggestions." Mrs. Chen pauses. "But that reminds me, our class contribution probably should be a physical object or paper-based. As strange as it may sound, who knows what kind of technology they may have then? We need to make sure it is easy to view without a device."

She chuckles. "For instance, in my childhood, we had floppy disks. That was about twenty-five years ago, and you two probably have no idea what I am talking about."

I push my eyebrows together. I hadn't considered that. I'm also trying to picture what a floppy disk looks like. Maybe it's like a round disk that is as wobbly as a baby seal flopping around on the beach.

Mrs. Chen stands up. "I'll let you two brainstorm and get to know each other better. I'll be back in a bit. I trust you'll behave."

When Mrs. Chen leaves, Jessica and I just stare at each other for almost a minute. Then I clear my throat. "Do you have any ideas?"

Jessica glances down at her paper and scrunches up her face. "Maybe a book with our writing?"

"What about artwork or photo collages?" I reply.

Jessica taps her chin. "Or it could be both. We could make it like a magazine. Something where everyone could write or draw what fifth grade was like."

"That's a good idea," I reply, trying not to sound surprised. It's actually a good idea.

Jessica sort of shrugs. "Thanks. I think I want to be an editor one day. My aunt is one, and she lives in New York City."

"Cool!" I reply. "I think I want to be an oceanographer, but I also love art."

Jessica giggles a little. "Everyone knows *that*, Stella."

I turn a little *roja* with anger. I knew Jessica would revert to her old ways.

Then Jessica stops giggling. "I mean . . . that's not a bad thing, though."

My *roja* face begins to fade away as she continues, "It's good that you know what you want to be."

I study her face, trying to see if she's smirking. I think she wasn't trying to be mean, but it's a little hard to know. I give her the benefit of the doubt and say, "I'm applying to a magnet middle school for art and science."

Jessica raises her eyebrows. "Wow. Umm . . . is Stanley going, too?"

I sit up taller. "No, he's not."

Jessica looks very pleased. Then she says, "It will be weird for you not to have him and Jenny in your classes."

To my surprise, she sounds sincere. Maybe I'm misjudging her.

I nod. "Yeah. I'm so used to seeing everyone here every day. It's going to be strange."

Jessica pouts her lip a bit. "My best friend, Michelle, is moving. Her family is leaving for Atlanta. Her dad got a new job, and they're staying here to let Michelle finish the school year. I was excited to go to middle school with her, but I guess that's not happening."

Michelle wasn't the nicest to me either in third grade, but I don't say that aloud. Jessica appears upset. If I'm going to believe that Jessica has changed, it's better to say something nice. So, trying my best, I reply, "I'm sorry. That's rough, but if you're really BFFs, you will be fine."

At least, that's what I hope for Jenny and me.

I certainly never thought I'd feel bad for Jessica, but I can tell she feels the same way I do. Now that we're in fifth grade, we're on the edge of all these big changes. While so many of them are exciting, not knowing how things will pan out is a little scary. It's like taking a deep dive into the dark ocean. I can't help but be reminded of Sylvia Earle. She made one of the deepest dives ever at 1,250 feet below the surface in a *JIM* suit with only a small light to guide her way. I think if Sylvia Earle can

do that alone, we'll survive middle school. Then it hits me. I realize Sylvia Earle would be the perfect person to write my application essay about! She is a trailblazer and an oceanographer, just like I aspire to be. I jot it down in my notebook. Whew, one less thing to worry about.

Jessica and I plan our idea together until Mrs. Chen returns. It's not that bad talking to Jessica. Maybe she is different now, just like Stanley said. Although I don't like how often she asked about him during our meeting. I think she might like him, which is weird to me. However, I ignore that, at least for right now. Making a project for the time capsule is the most important thing. I don't know if Jessica and I feel like friends, but I definitely feel like we can work together.

Chapter Twelve

Weekly appointments are a tradition
Mom started a while back. It was a way to make sure we
have fun every Friday night as a family. She always puts
it in her schedule to make sure nothing ever gets in the
way of our tradition. Now that I have my own schedule, I do it, too. However, our weekly appointments
have changed some over the years. At first, it used to
be only Mom, Nick, and me, but now, more and more
people join. This week I have Jenny sleeping over, and
our neighbors, Diego and Izzy, are joining us for pizza.
Even Nick's girlfriend, Erika, said she'd stop by.

When I think about how many people are going
to attend, I start counting my fingers. By the time I

get to my seventh finger, I exclaim, "Mom, that's seven people for pizza! We're going to need, like, two pizzas!"

Mom laughs. "We're going to need three pizzas. We should invite Linda, and you know your *hermano. El puede comer una pizza entera.*"

I start giggling. It's true, Nick *can* eat a whole pizza by himself! Although it would be even funnier if he tried stuffing it into his mouth all at once like a pelican.

Before everyone comes over, I walk Ramona and Biscuit. When I first walked the two of them together, I was a little afraid that Biscuit would be jealous that I have my own dog. After all, it used to be only him and me on our walks. Thankfully, he adores Ramona. When we're together, he even acts as if he needs to protect us. It's hilarious, too, because Ramona and I are both bigger than he is.

When I get back to Linda's house, I notice a FOR SALE sign out front. I must have missed it earlier. I frown. I guess Linda is finally moving. I knew it was coming, but this sign makes it official.

When I step back inside, I let Biscuit off his leash and find Linda in the kitchen messing with a roll of packing tape.

"Linda, my mom wants to know if you want to come over tonight for pizza."

"I could use a break from this packing tape." She tosses it onto the counter. "It always sticks back together."

I'm surprised to see Linda frustrated. She's the one who usually comforts me. She must be stressed from packing boxes.

I pick up the roll. "Let me help. I'm an expert at finding where the tape has stuck back to itself."

"My heroine," she replies, sounding grateful.

"When are you moving, Linda?" I ask as I flip the tape over.

Linda sighs. "Not for a little while, honey. I need to sell my house first, but I did finally find a place nearby that I'm going to buy. It has a private pool and clubhouse. I can invite guests, too."

"Really?" I reply excitedly. As a future oceanographer, it would be great to have a place to practice my swimming. Maybe they will have cookies and lemonade, too. That would be a refreshing treat after a big swim.

She nods. "I'm trying to figure out what to donate and what to keep. It's a little hard to downsize when you're my age and have accumulated a lot of memories."

She looks around her home; her face is a little sad. I give her a hug.

"I'll help," I say. "We will all help."

"Thanks, sugarplum." She claps her hands and continues, "Now, let's go eat some pizza."

Linda puts on her coat, and we head next door to

my house. When we arrive, I whisper to Mom, "We have eight people tonight. That's practically a party!"

She does a quick cha-cha move. "*¡Una fiesta!*"

Then, right on cue, the doorbell rings. First, Jenny arrives with her sleeping bag, followed by Diego and Izzy. Nick leaves to go pick up Erika and the pizzas from his work. While we wait, Mom talks with the grown-ups in the kitchen. It's mostly about Linda's move and putting her house up for sale. It sounds awfully complicated.

Meanwhile, Izzy, Jenny, and I hang out in the living room with the dogs. Izzy is older than Jenny and me. She just started eighth grade and is officially a teenager.

"Oh, I like your nails," Jenny says to Izzy. Izzy waves her fingers at us. Her nails are striped with sparkles.

"Thanks! My mom takes me and my friends to get manicures every once in a while."

Izzy's parents are divorced like my parents. But unlike Nick and me, she splits half her time with her mom and the other half with her dad, Diego.

"Wow," I reply. That sounds so grown up. I look down at my nails. Jenny has painted my nails at sleepovers a handful of times. Are manicures something middle schoolers should do?

"How do you like eighth grade, by the way?" asks Jenny, nibbling on candy corn. Mom thought since it's Halloween weekend we should have some candy treats for our guests.

"Eighth grade is by far the best grade in middle school."

"Why?" I ask.

"Sixth grade was a little tough," Izzy replies. "You go from being the oldest kid in the elementary school to all of a sudden being the youngest. The eighth graders seem so big then, too. Also, there are new kids from different schools, and some of them are not so nice. Now that I'm in eighth grade, I don't have to worry about being the smallest anymore."

I gulp. Is that what sixth grade is going to be like? I forgot I'd be the youngest again. Will I be in a school surrounded by bullies? Suddenly, I imagine being a male walrus in one of those nature documentaries, fighting other male walruses for dominance. I don't want to be trampled over. I look over at Jenny. She looks a little nervous, too.

Izzy sees our faces and then quickly adds, "But sixth grade is great, too. You can make new friends. Plus, you have a locker and switch classes. You're not stuck in one room all day long."

That does sound like it could be fun.

Jenny says, "Hopefully we can have our lockers next to each other. I've always wanted to slip notes like they do in the movies."

I gulp again. I still haven't told Jenny about the

magnet school! Maybe I should tell her now. But before I can say anything, Izzy asks, "Oh, Jenny, are you applying to the magnet school with Stella?"

My face turns white. My big secret is out. Jenny turns and looks at me. "What magnet school?"

Izzy realizes she has spilled my secret and looks embarrassed. But it's not her fault. I should have told Jenny sooner.

I take a deep breath and confess. "Ms. Benedetto recommended this special middle school that I should apply to. It's called the Chicago Art and Science Magnet School. She's been recommending it to students who are really good artists. But the application is really complicated, and a lot of kids apply. I probably won't get in."

I try to downplay it so it sounds like I'm not excited.

"Does that mean you might not be going to the same middle school as me?" Jenny asks, looking a little hurt. "And how long have you known?"

"A month or so," I reply as I turn bright *roja*. Then, like a dam, I break and tell her everything. "I meant to

tell you earlier, but I didn't really realize that we might go to separate schools until I started applying. I was just so excited that I didn't think about that. Then I didn't know how to bring it up."

Jenny looks at the ground. I can tell I've hurt her feelings. Izzy even puts her arm around Jenny to comfort her.

Suddenly, I get a brilliant idea because maybe Jenny and I don't have to go to different schools. "Wait here," I say.

I quickly run upstairs and find the Art and Science pamphlet. I'm practically out of breath when I place it in Jenny's hand.

"You can apply, too! It's a school for arts, and you love to dance." I continue, "I can help you with the application, too. It's due March 15, so you'll have plenty of time."

"Maybe, Stella," Jenny says as she eyes the pamphlet. "I'll look into it with my mom."

Izzy breaks the silence. "It really doesn't matter if you two go to different schools. You're best friends forever. I'm still BFF with my friend from my old neighborhood. We've been in different schools for years."

I know Izzy still talks to her best friend, Sam, all the time. But I'm a little afraid that it won't be like that for Jenny and me. What if Jenny changes her mind?

Thankfully, we're interrupted by the front door opening as Nick and Erika walk in with the pizzas.

"Pizza is here," Nick mumbles while chewing on a slice. By the look of it, he's already had a few. Luckily, Mom was smart and ordered an extra pizza.

Erika sits down beside us. "What are you girls talking about?"

"Nothing," I reply.

She seems confused by our silence. Then Izzy
quickly says, "Let's grab some pizza before your brother
eats it all."

The rest of the night is better. We eat and play
games, and after a while, Jenny seems to be laughing
and having a good time like a typical Friday night. By
the time we go to sleep, it seems like everything is back
to normal. But as I turn off the light in my room, I see
Jenny in her sleeping bag staring at the pamphlet. Even
in the dark, I can tell she's frowning.

Chapter Thirteen

Most of the leaves have changed from green to bright, warm colors by the time we have our Sea Musketeers fall fundraiser. It's sort of a mild day, which is great because we're planting trees today. It's not many trees, but with some of the previous money we raised, we were able to buy a few trees from the Arbor Day Foundation. Our hope is that people will donate more money to the Sea Musketeers once they see us in action. This way we can fund Plant a Billion Trees and the Billion Oyster Project, too.

I have to admit I was a little nervous with it being the first weekend in November, that planting trees wouldn't be a good idea. But to my surprise, Nick discovered in our research that fall is actually a great time to plant trees. Apparently, since summer can be so hot, it can be too stressful for the trees if you plant them then or in spring. However, if you plant them in fall, they get an extra season to adapt and grow. Plus, they just hibernate in winter like some fish do. Since we haven't had a strong frost yet, we head over to a park near Mariel's house for our event. The best part is, it's so close by that she and her parents can check on our trees.

First, we set up our typical fundraiser table. I start to arrange baked goods for sale, posters with information, and more importantly, our pledge to cut back on plastics. Unfortunately, we don't have Linda's crocheted tote bags this time. She's too busy getting ready for the move to her smaller place. She promised to have them for the next event, but I'm a little worried that may not be true.

"How can I help, Stella?" Gabby asks enthusiastically. She's dressed in green and wearing little seahorse earrings.

I invited Gabby to volunteer at the fundraiser

because I knew she'd be thrilled. But really, the bigger reason is I feel bad. I still haven't asked the Sea Musketeers if we should add new members. With so many things changing, I just want the Sea Musketeers to stay the same. Gabby keeps asking at school, of course. I thought this invitation could buy me some more time. Also, it helps me to figure out whether it would be strange to add a new member to the group.

"Gabby, you could get people to sign the pledge," I reply as I put on my gardening gloves.

She jumps up and down. "You got it, boss!" she replies, and runs toward the table.

It takes two Sea Musketeers and one adult to plant a tree. While the trees are barely taller than me, planting trees is hard work. Not only do you have to dig a giant hole, you have to cover them up with soil and mulch, too. Thankfully, we have Kristen's parents and Mr. Kyle to help us out.

"Guess what?" whispers Mariel to me. "Mr. Kyle is going to write me a letter of recommendation for Chicago Art and Science."

Having Mr. Kyle write a letter of recommendation is a great idea. He was one of our camp leaders at the Shedd summer camp. It might be nice to have someone who can talk about my experience with the Sea Musketeers for the application.

"Do you think he'd write one for me?" I reply in a normal voice.

"I do," she whispers.

I wonder why Mariel keeps whispering, but then I remember our earlier pact.

"I think it's okay to talk about the application with the group. I even told Jenny." I elbow her jokingly. "Unless you really feel like whispering."

Mariel replies in a normal voice, "Whew, thanks. It was getting hard to whisper. What did Jenny think?"

"Umm . . ." I nervously clear my throat. "I think she might apply, too."

I look over at Jenny. She's laughing with Gabby at the table. Jenny and I haven't spoken about the application since the night she found out. Everything has seemed fine. School is so busy and she has dance lessons, too, so we haven't had an opportunity to talk. But deep down, I know that's not true. I guess it's a conversation I am putting off.

After we finish planting, I have a quick chat with Mr. Kyle about the letter. He happily agrees. As I head back to the table, Gabby runs up to me.

"This is better than I could ever imagine."

I smile. Then she asks, "When can I be a member?"

"Umm . . . we'll vote on it soon," I reply, half lying.

I'm sure we'll vote on it soon once I finally discuss it with the group. I turn away so she can't see my guilty expression.

Gabby squeals with delight and folds her hands together.

"Stella, while I was standing there, I've had some thoughts about the pledge, too."

I cross my arms. "What do you mean . . . ?"

"Well, cutting down on plastic is great, but we can do other things to protect the oceans. Maybe we include a few more tips. Like how you should walk or ride your bike when you can instead of driving a car. The gasoline from cars pollutes our waterways. Or did you know that you can save water by taking a shower instead of a bath?"

I stand there silently. The pledge is perfect as it is. We came up with it at the Shedd Aquarium summer camp with Mr. Kyle. Why would we change anything?

However, Gabby's eyes are as round as Ramona's when she's begging. I muster a response.

"Those are good ideas. Maybe it could be a separate pledge instead."

"It'll be Gabby's pledge!" she says, waving her hand in the air.

"Sure," I reply. "For right now, make sure we have people sign the Sea Musketeers pledge, though."

Gabby salutes me and goes back to the table.

Toward the end of the fundraiser, when we've either eaten or sold all our baked goods, we step out into a group huddle. I was worried Gabby would ask about being a member again, but her dad picked her up early. Logan speaks first.

"It's only a few more weeks till the holidays. How would you all feel about taking a winter break this year? Maybe a week before school break, and then we can all start back up after New Year's?"

My eyes grow big. If everyone gets busier, they might not even meet after New Year's and that might mean the end of the Sea Musketeers as we know it. I want to exclaim, "No way!" I try to think of a nicer way to say it, but before I can respond, Kristen says, "I think that would be a good idea. I have my first midterms in middle school this year."

Stanley replies, "Wow, that's a little scary."

Kristen pulls at her braids in frustration. "Middle school is a lot of work."

Other group members share reasons we should take a break. Logan has family coming into town, and Mariel is leaving for Florida soon with her family. Strangely, no one mentioned these things last year. We decide to take a vote. Everyone raises their hand except for me, but I end up raising it in the end. I don't want to cause a scene. It's starting to feel like this club isn't anyone's number one priority, except for me and Gabby. And Gabby isn't even a member yet. Could the Sea Musketeers be fading away? This has been one of my big dreams for a while, and I'm not ready to say goodbye.

Instead of chatting with the rest of the group, I kick a rock on the ground back and forth until Nick picks me up.

"How was saving the world?" he asks as I take my spot in the back seat.

"The planet is saved," I reply sarcastically. I don't really feel like talking about the meeting.

He chuckles and turns up the radio. It's a little loud, which makes it hard to talk to him. I spy around in the car instead. His stinky karate bag is by my feet. I waft the air a bit to get rid of the smell. Then I notice some mail beside me. There's a catalog to the local art store, which is exciting. Underneath it is a large envelope. It looks fancy. I think maybe it's from the magnet school, but when I look more closely, I see it's from a university in California and it's addressed to Nick.

I tap the back of Nick's seat. "Why do you have mail from a college?"

He lowers the radio and says, "I think when you sign up for the PSATs, they put your name on a mailing list for colleges. I received some other ones already."

"But you're only a sophomore in high school!" I exclaim.

He shrugs.

"Well, my PSATs are this year in the spring. SATs are my junior year, and you apply for college early into your senior year. By then, you need to know which schools you'd like to apply for. Jason is planning to visit some colleges with his mom in the summer."

My mouth drops open. "Really?"

He tugs at the brim of his baseball cap. "It's not really that far away when you think of it like that."

I feel my stomach flip. Everything seems to be changing all at once, but I didn't consider this big change for Nick. Before I know it, Nick could move to California or to some college even farther away, like in Australia. Then I won't see him every day. Nick is my older brother, but he's also like my second dad. He always helps me when I'm in a pickle. From school to struggling with being an immigrant, he's always been there. Not to mention, he's also the unofficial Sea Musketeers mentor. How will I survive without him? How will the club, which seems to be slipping through my fingers, survive, too? I slump back in my seat. This whole year, all I've wanted to do is leap toward the future. But now for the first time, I just want things to remain the same. Maybe I could invent a machine to freeze time just for a little while. I hope this magnet school has impressive futuristic technology, because I am going to need help making it.

Chapter Fourteen

The holidays are low-key this year.
Since *mis abuelos* visited us after our citizenship ceremony in the spring, they decided to stay in Mexico
and visit us next year. Plus, Stanley and Jenny both
went away with their families for winter break, so it
was mostly just Mom, Nick, and me. While it was fun
to make *champurrado* and play games with my family
at Christmas, it was a sad reminder of how I may see
less of my closest friends next year if I go to a different
school. However, I loved that I got a break from all my
application work and worries. At least for a little while.

That all changes in January, once the holidays are
over. It's 100 percent back to reality when Mom and

I finally take a tour of the magnet school. It's an open house event, and the school is packed with other kids and their parents, which makes me nervous about my chances.

"What do you think?" says Mom, staring at the tall building.

CHICAGO ART AND SCIENCE MAGNET SCHOOL

"It's big!" I reply. It's much bigger than Arlington Heights Elementary, but honestly, I feel a little confused. As excited as I was, I was kind of hoping I wouldn't like the school. My life would be way easier if I just went to the regular middle school with my friends.

I watch the kids walking in, hoping to see Chris and Mariel. It's hard to spot them among the crowd. I do notice one girl who has electric-blue hair. That's really unique! Maybe I could do that for my middle school hairstyle. It might be tricky to convince Mom, though.

"¡*Qué lindo!* There is so much light," Mom says, elbowing me gently in the side.

My eyes wander around the main hallway. I'm a little speechless. This school looks like a museum! But what good is a nice-looking school without my friends?

We begin the tour with a visit to the science wing, and I gasp when I see a giant aquarium between the different lab rooms. I read the little plaque right below it.

Mom places her arm around me. "¡*Mira*, Stella! It was donated by the friends of the Shedd."

I shrug. Even I can admit that's pretty impressive. But still, no friends. Three stars out of five.

As we walk around, I spy a lot of interesting science equipment. I don't know what half of it does, but I do recognize some signs for coding. Logan has started to talk about it at our club meetings, when he's not mentioning shark facts.

"Do you have any questions about the science department?" a boy, who looks to be Izzy's age, asks us.

Without thinking, I ask, "Are there classes on the ocean and the environment?"

He replies excitedly, "Definitely. That's a hot topic at this school. We actually volunteered with the Shedd to explore and preserve living islands in the Chicago River. These islands help create and protect biodiversity."

"That's so cool." I glance over at Mom, who is smiling.

I grin from ear to ear. This might be a pretty good school for me. Four stars.

Mom and I visit the art area last. I'm blown away by all the types of art making. I could build sculptures on the pottery wheels and make prints like van Gogh

with their printmaking machines, not to mention the easels and fashion mannequins. It's more than I could imagine. In fact, this might be the perfect school for me. Six million out of five stars!

After we finish the tour, Mom attends a brief Q&A with administrators in the auditorium while I stare at all the art in the halls. Maybe my artwork could hang up here one day.

Suddenly, I see someone walking down the hallway. She has long, straight black hair and a backpack just like Jenny's. I follow her for a second, hoping it's her, but when she turns around, it's not Jenny. I wonder if Jenny is applying to the magnet school. This reminds me that I need to talk to her. That's one conversation I can't avoid for much longer.

We leave the school, and I feel like I'm floating. Is this a dream? I hear you're supposed to pinch yourself to see if you're dreaming. When I do it, I confirm that this is real. That pinch hurt!

Mom begins to speak.

"You'd get an amazing education there."

I hug Mom. "I have to make the application the best it could ever be."

Mom agrees. "Maybe I can get some of the tech guys at the radio station to help out with the video part of the application."

I clasp my hands together. Mom is a manager at some Spanish radio stations. They have all this high-tech recording equipment for the DJs. It's way better than we have at home. I exclaim, "*¡Sí, por favor!*"

"This school will be an adjustment, though," Mom says. "I was speaking to the principal, and all the students are bused in. You'd have to wake up a little earlier than normal to catch the bus."

I don't mind waking up earlier. I am sometimes the first one awake, especially now that we have Ramona. But if I'm taking a bus, I won't be riding to school with Mom. That means I'll see her less.

"You can't drive me?" I ask.

She shakes her head. "It would be too much traffic for this neighborhood."

I scrunch my face.

Mom sees my expression. "But imagine all the cool things you'll see in the morning. You'll see the sunrise on Lake Michigan and meet more kids this way. You may make a friend before you even arrive on the first day of school."

"That's true," I reply, somewhat convinced.

"We'll also save money on gas," she continues. "I'll just take the Metra stop closer to home instead of driving."

Mom does have good points. That *is* better for the environment. Suddenly, I come up with a great solution.

"Okay," I say. "It will be worth it. But we have to schedule more weekly appointments to spend time together."

I put my hand out to Mom. "Deal?"

Mom then extends her hand. "*Acuerdo*."

Just before we get into the car, we shake on it.

Chapter Fifteen

It's after school, and Jessica and I are reviewing some of the student submissions for the time capsule. Since Jessica and I have been working well together in past meetings, Mrs. Chen trusts us to work alone on the project today. Still, Mrs. Chen stays in the room and grades assignments nearby in case we need her.

As we sort through the stack, I grab one of my favorite entries. We told the class the submissions should either sum up fifth grade or an experience in elementary school. We also made it open, meaning it could be art or written, whatever they'd like, just as long as they got it to us quickly. We're hoping to get all the entries approved by March or April because we'd like to design it and send it to a printer so we can bind it all together like a real magazine!

"This one is great!" I point proudly. "Stanley made this cool timeline about all the NASA adventures from our time in school."

"We've got to keep that one," Jessica says with googly eyes. She gets that look whenever I mention Stanley. I don't know if Stanley feels the same about her, though.

Jessica picks up a drawing. "This one is awful." She starts snickering. "Do we have to include everyone's?"

I look at the drawing. It's not the best drawing I've seen, but it's not exactly nice to make fun of it either.

I pause to come up with the best response.

"I think everyone should contribute something. Maybe we can ask them to resubmit or try a different way, like a collage instead."

Jessica rolls her eyes. "I guess so. I'll put it in the maybe folder for now."

While I've been pleasantly surprised by how much

I've gotten along with Jessica, she's still a little judg-mental at times. But I also really admire her orga-nizational system for the project. She has multiple folders for all types of categories. Even Mom would be impressed.

People can be interesting, I guess. They can change in some ways, but maybe not as much in other ways. If I had to compare Jessica to an aquatic creature, I'd say she is like one of the "vegetarian piranhas" they found in southeastern Michigan. They look menac-ing, but really these fish just prefer to eat plants. I think Jessica is mostly harmless and only appears mean sometimes.

Still, while Jessica has changed, one thing is clear. We're never going to become best friends forever, not like Jenny and me. Then I'm reminded, I need to talk to Jenny about the magnet school. I look at the clock. She should be home from dance class by the time I'm fin-ished with the time capsule meeting. I am determined to finally deal with this.

After I'm home from school, I give Jenny a call.

I feel my heart race a little as the phone rings. Thankfully, her mom answers quickly and hands Jenny her phone.

I say in sort of a high-pitched voice, "Hi, Jenny. How was dance class?"

She replies, "Good! I'm all sweaty. Ms. Charlton had us trying new choreography for the spring recital. It was hard."

She asks me about Jessica and the time capsule. When I tell her what happened in today's meeting, she doesn't sound surprised.

"I still don't trust her, but I guess I can be nice to her."

"Same," I reply, and then I finally ask the question I've been meaning to say aloud for a while. "So have you worked on your application for the magnet school? I keep meaning to ask you. It's due in, like, six weeks."

There is a long pause.

"Stella, I'd love to go to the same middle school, but . . ."

Oh no, I'm not going to get the response I wanted.

She continues, "I just don't want to go to the magnet school. I want to stick with the regular school."

"Oh," I reply. "Did you see that they have a dance program?"

Jenny sighs. "I know, but Arlington Heights Middle School is closer to home and to my dance studio. I love Ms. Charlton and my friends there."

I feel a little choked up. I guess she likes them more than me. Still, I manage to say a polite response.

"I understand."

"Thank you, Stella. I'm so excited for you, and I really hope you get in."

I reply thank you, and we quickly hang up the phone. I hang out in my room, trying to work on my application essay on Sylvia Earle until Mom gets home. Instead, I just lie on my bed and stare at the ceiling, with Ramona by my side. She can always sense when I need a little extra comfort.

"*¿Estás triste?*" Mom asks if I'm sad as she enters my room.

I nod. "Jenny isn't applying to the magnet school."

She sits beside me. "I'm sorry, *mi amor*. It will be okay."

Mom stands back up. "I'm going to change out of my work clothes. I'll be right back, and we can talk about it more."

While she's gone, I sit and pout. Ramona begins to sniff my wrist and the best-friend bracelet Jenny made me in third grade. Jenny has made one every year. I have four in total, but this is my favorite one.

Then I notice all my Sea Musketeers photos on my bulletin board. Jenny is in every single photograph. Even though she isn't a future oceanographer like me, she has been to most of the meetings and all the fundraisers. All because saving the oceans is important to me. Just like how I've been to many of her dance recitals.

Suddenly, it's like I'm finally seeing things clearly. Jenny and I have overcome challenges in the past. I'm also sure there will be more in the future, but what matters most is we're always here for each other. That's what real best friends do.

I get a great idea. I run to Mom's room, and Ramona follows.

"Mom, can I invite Jenny over?"

She looks surprised. "*Claro que sí*," she replies. "I take it you're feeling better?"

"*Sí*, I was just being silly."

Mom gives me a hug. "We all have our moments."

I call Jenny back. Luckily, she answers her mom's cell on the first ring.

"Hi, Jenny, do you want to come over and help me with my application? I'm stuck on the essay."

Jenny replies, "Of course! I thought you'd never ask."

I beam with joy. I'm lucky to have a friend like Jenny. She's my BFF, and that's never going to change.

Chapter Sixteen

It's a cold Sunday in February. The per-fect weather to be curled up with some blankets and a drawing pad. It's only a few weeks until March 15, when the magnet school application is due, and I've been making solid progress.

We finally shot my video. We did it at the radio station with some of the radio production team's help. They made it look as professional as a television show. In fact, I sat behind a table like a news reporter. I even sort of sound like one in the video, which I hope is okay.

Then Jenny helped me edit and revise my Sylvia Earle essay. I made sure to include everything I admire about her, like how she was the first female chief scientist of the NOAA and named a "hero of the planet" by *Time* magazine. While I'm technically done with my video and essay application, it feels like they're both missing something. It's almost like a dish that needs a little *sabor*, or flavor, to make it feel special. Unfortunately, I don't know what that is.

Thankfully, I have the last part to work on in the meantime, the art project. I saved it for last since I knew it would be the most fun. Plus, Ms. Benedetto and Mr. Foster were away on their honeymoon at the start of quarter, and I had to wait till they got back for an inspiring brainstorm session. With their suggestions, I decide to do a drawing of my favorite sea creatures. That way I could incorporate my two interests together, art and science. Of course, I must include my betta fish, Pancho, front and center. He was my first in-person introduction to aquatic animals and jumpstarted my whole fascination with aquariums. Once I had my own tiny fishbowl at home, I had to experience the big, giant aquariums like the ones at Shedd, too!

I study Pancho carefully as I draw him. I use all the blue-colored pencils, like indigo and cobalt, to capture his likeness. However, as I'm drawing him, I notice that his fins look less like beautiful silk than they did before. One is even a tiny bit ragged. Is my best fish buddy, Pancho, looking older? I've had him for a few years now, and who knows how old he was when we got him? I begin to worry. I think about asking Nick, who is studying in his room. Then I spy the laptop.

Since I'm ten now, Mom lets me borrow it unsupervised, but I'm only supposed to use it to write my essay. However, this is urgent! I quickly search online and find a website about betta fish. It describes all the qualities of an older fish. Some of the descriptions sound just like him. He has a ragged fin, and he seems to be moving less. I run back to examine Pancho to see if there are any more signs. My nose is practically pressed against the glass. He's barely moving as I try to study his scales for humps or white spots. I tap the glass to see if he'll move, and he doesn't!

"NICK!" I cry out. Ramona jumps up and barks.

Nick runs over. "What's wrong? Are you hurt?"

I begin to whimper. "Pancho isn't moving, and I read this website. It sounds like he's getting old. What if he dies? Do you know CPR?"

I start to imagine how a person would even do CPR on a fish. Meanwhile, Nick puts on his serious face and inspects Pancho.

"Hey, man." He taps on the glass. "How are you doing?"

Suddenly, Pancho does a giant swirl around his bowl. He looks like his young, spunky self.

I jump up and down with happiness. Then I immediately pick up Ramona and pull Nick into a group hug.

Nick usually groans when I hug him, but this time he hugs me back.

"Thank you, *hermano*!" I exclaim.

"No problem," he replies. "Pancho might be getting older, but I think he's still young at heart. He has a while before you have to worry about him."

I let out a sigh of relief as I hold Ramona.

Nick looks at the clock, then at me. "I could use a break from homework. Do you want to get some ice cream?"

I look outside at the gray wintry sky. "But it's so cold outside, Nick."

Nick shrugs. "Ice cream is perfect at any time. We'll just bundle up more. C'mon."

I nod. Nick gets permission from Mom while I put on my puffy jacket, beanie, and gloves.

"Does Mom want to go?" I ask as we head toward the door.

Nick shakes his head. "Nah, this is just me and you. We just have to bring her back a surprise scoop."

I squeal. Even though it's just a five-minute drive from our house, nothing is more exciting than spending some time with Nick. Especially since he's been

busier with Erika, school, PSATs, and all his respon-
sibilities.

It's mostly silent in the car. We're just enjoying
the sound of Nick's music. When I'm in the car with
Mom, it's either salsa or classical. With Nick, though,
he likes a range from rock to hip-hop. I don't know
what music I necessarily like, but I figure if Nick likes
it, it must be good.

After we select our ice cream flavors, we grab a table
at Oberweis to sit down and enjoy our icy treats.

"How's your ice cream, Nick?"

He takes a giant bite. He went with Rocky Road,
which is unusual.

"It's good! This is Erika's favorite," he says. "I'd put
it up there with cookies and cream."

I tighten my mouth to the side. Another thing that
is changing. Nick always gets cookies and cream, but
apparently, he might have a new favorite flavor.

Nick taps my arm. "What's that face about?"

I sigh. "It just feels like so much is changing." Then
it's like all my worries come out at once. "I was so

excited about applying for the school, and I still am, but going to a different school is scary. And everyone in the Sea Musketeers is getting busy, so I don't even know if that's going to keep happening. Then you're going off to college so soon. I don't want any other changes. Zilch, please."

Nick gives a side smile. "That's a lot to keep bottled up inside, kiddo."

On one hand, I want to cry, but on the other hand, I feel lighter just saying it aloud.

"Yeah," I reply. I start laughing a little, too.

Nick chuckles. "I definitely relate to what you're feeling. Change is a mixed bag. It can be good, exciting, but some changes are just plain bad. You've got to sort of deal with it and try to enjoy the good ones. Ice cream helps, too."

Nick's certainly right about ice cream, and I take another spoonful. Then I ask him something that has been bothering me for a while.

"Nick, are you planning to go really far away for college, like California?"

He shakes his head. "Nah, college is expensive, and it's way cheaper to stay in state."

Then I remember a fact about sea turtles. Adult male sea turtles never leave the ocean, only the female sea turtles. That's because the females must leave to lay the eggs on land. This always felt a little sad to me. The ocean is awesome, but so is being on land. I want Nick to have a full experience of what's out there if he wants it.

"You're not just staying here because of me and Mom, right?" I ask.

He replies, "I'm staying here in Chicago because it's the best city and has some of the best education. It's a no-brainer."

I smile happily, then ask, "Do you know what you want to study in college?"

Nick rests his chin in his hands. "I've been thinking about teaching."

"I didn't know that." I feel a little shocked, but I guess I had never asked him before either.

He continues, "My European history teacher, Mr. Maigur, is really inspiring, and he looks like he is having the time of his life. I think it would be really cool to be like him."

Nick sounds like such a grown-up. I think he could be a great teacher, too. He's helped me with many of my projects at school. He's always patient, too.

"I'm excited for you," I say.

"Likewise, sis." Then he gives me a tap on the top of my beanie. "I know you're nervous about all the changes, but you're going to do great in middle school. Whatever school it ends up being. The world is your oyster, or whatever sea creature you want it to be."

I laugh. "I think I'd go with a dolphin. They seem very smart and friendly."

"Wise decision," he replies. Then he takes another bite from his cone.

On the car ride home, Nick surprises me by playing my favorite song, "Octopus's Garden" by the Beatles.

Nick discovered it when I was working on my third-grade animal project. Back then, we used to play it nonstop, but it's been a while since we've listened to it together. I immediately turn up the volume, and we sing at the top of our lungs all the way back home.

Chapter Seventeen

I'm in the living room, staring at the chalkboard schedule Mom made to help us stay organized. My eyes can't believe it. It's March 1. While I'm excited for spring, it also means my application is due in two weeks.

Mom senses I'm a little wound up.

"*¿Quieres ir por un paseo con Ramona?*" she asks, throwing her arm around me.

Usually, I'd love to take a stroll with Mom and Ramona, but now is not the time.

I shake my head. "I'm going to double-check my application."

"Okay, *mi amor*." Mom kisses the top of my head. "Let me know if you need my help."

I give her a hug and head up to my room to review it all for the millionth time. My artwork is really good, but I feel like my video and essay are so boring! I don't think they'll really stand out among the pack. But I can't figure out what is missing! I cuddle with Ramona while I stare around the room.

My time capsule entry catches my eye. I did a photo collage of the Sea Musketeers at work and wrote in big letters, *Fifth graders care about the oceans.*

As I study the group's faces, including Gabby, who snuck into our fall fundraiser photo, I start thinking about these past few years. The plastic pledge is a super important part of the Sea Musketeers and a big accomplishment, but I realize that is not what matters the most. It's the people in the pictures. The same people who, along with my other friendships, have helped me grow and change over the years. Maybe that's why the video is boring, because it's just a list of things I've done over the years. It's like watching someone read aloud a grocery list, except less delicious-sounding.

With renewed inspiration, I run downstairs.

"Can I borrow your phone and tripod, Mom?"

"Of course," she replies. Her right eyebrow is raised, but she stands up from the couch ready to help. Once we set up the camera, she leaves me alone in my room without saying a word.

"Okay, let's do this, Ramona," I say to my sleeping dog as I press RECORD.

With a deep breath, I begin. For the first time, I speak freely to the camera and from the heart. I don't need note cards this time, because I know what to say.

I start with mentioning a few of my accomplishments, like the mural, awards, and the Sea Musketeers. Then I move to something more real. Because even though those are important, my most important accomplishments have been the changes inside me. I share about my shyness and how I'd turn as *roja* as a tomato whenever I was put on the spot. And how fear held me back. Then luckily it changed in third grade, when I discovered I had a voice and something worth saying. That made my confidence skyrocket, and I now realize there is nothing better than making new friends. With my growing determination and team-work, the Sea Musketeers have accomplished ocean-size things. As my dreams have become bigger with time, I've learned when to ask for help from my family and friends. And in return, I've learned the importance of being a supportive and understanding friend. Last, I finish with how I'd love to attend the magnet school, but no matter what, I'm excited to see how I'll continue to evolve in the coming years.

When I finish, I press STOP on the camera. I feel goose bumps. Even though it wasn't shot on a fancy camera or a green screen, I don't think I could have done any better than this.

I'm about to run downstairs to tell Mom about my new video when I remember something important. Chris mentioned he is writing his application essay on his dad because he is his hero. While I love Sylvia Earle, she's no Perla Díaz. Meaning, my mom is the absolute best and my hero, too! She always reminds me how I am stronger than I think and encourages me with everything I do. It's been so obvious! My essay should be about her. I close my door and get started on writing my improved essay. When I'm nearly done, I hear a tap on my door.

"Everything okay here?" Mom asks with a curious expression.

"It's great," I reply. "I rewrote my paper and re-recorded my video."

Mom's eyes grow big. She's about to say something when I interrupt her.

"I know it's dramatic, but they were boring and weren't really me." I twirl my curls. "Can I share them with you?"

I watch Mom's face as she watches the video. I see a few pleased expressions, but she stays silent. Then I read the essay aloud to her. When I'm done, I lower my paper slowly. "What do you think, Mom? Do you think they're better?"

I peek over at her face. Her eyes look sparkly, and there is a huge smile. "They are perfect. *Magnífico*."

Then she gives me a big hug.

She whispers, "Don't grow up too quickly, promise?"

I hug her back even harder. "I won't."

Chapter Eighteen

Today's a big day at school. It's the day before my application is due, but more than that, it's my last opportunity to have it reviewed before we send it off. I have Mom drop me off a little early at school so I can get my teachers' input on the writing and drawing.

The hallways are quiet as I walk around. The only noise you can hear at first is my squeaky feet on the clean floor. As I turn a corner, I spy Mr. Don, who is mopping the floors. He's whistling a Beach Boys song to himself until he notices me.

"Hi, Stella! Be careful. It's a little slippery in this spot."

"I will!" I tiptoe carefully up to him. "Guess what? I'm applying to the Chicago Art and Science Magnet School!"

He whistles. "Wow. I know you'll get in! I still have my portrait hanging up in my house. I tell my kids and family that the famous Stella Díaz made it."

I turn a little *roja*. "Thanks, Mr. Don."

I made a portrait of him in fourth grade for the art

club's gallery show. We could choose any adult who works at the school, and I selected him because he's kind and remembers everyone's name. He was so helpful to me when he shared his experience of becoming a US citizen. I'm going to miss him at my new school, whatever it may be.

Then I wave goodbye and walk to Ms. Benedetto's class. She's sitting at her desk sipping coffee when I come in. Before she can even say hello, I open my makeshift portfolio case and pull out my application artwork.

"What do you think of my drawing for the magnet school?"

Ms. Benedetto rests her face in her hand. Her wedding band presses against her cheek. "I love it. It's fabulous."

"How do I take a picture of it, though?" I ask. "My mom and I weren't sure which was the best way."

She looks at her watch and stands up. "We've got time to scan this. Follow me."

We head to the art room, where Mr. Foster helps

us use a scanner. It takes a few scans to get the whole image, but then they magically piece it together on the computer. Before I know it, I have a digital image that looks as good as my drawing does in person.

"I'll email it to your mom." Ms. Benedetto picks up my drawing. "And I'll hold on to this. You can pick it up at art club today."

"*¡Gracias!*" I reply as I look at the wall clock. Yikes, I've got to run!

The next stop is my class. The bell rings before I can ask Mrs. Chen to look at my application essay. I try again at lunchtime. Unfortunately, she has a staff meeting then, so I'm not able to get her to review it then either. I have to wait all the way till the end of the day. It feels like the longest day of my life.

When the final bell rings, I jump in front of her desk.

"Can you read my application essay?" I ask, nearly out of breath.

"Of course."

I hand Mrs. Chen my paper. Before she starts

reading, she grabs a red pen. I gulp. That red pen is for grammar mistakes. Then she reads silently. I watch her face for any expression. There are a couple of small smiles. At least, I think so. Maybe she needs to sneeze. When she's done reading, she puts the cap back on the pen and hands it back to me.

"It's well done, Stella. You should be proud of yourself."

"Really? No mistakes?"

"Not that I could see, and I read it closely. You've really improved your grammar. They would be lucky to have you at that school."

I tap my feet with excitement. "Thank you, Mrs. Chen."

From her expression, I can tell she is proud of me. Mrs. Chen may be different from Ms. Benedetto, but I realize that's a good thing. She just had high expectations for me. Mrs. Chen helped me become a better writer. Because of her, I have a greater chance of getting into the school. I'm really glad she's my teacher this year.

I skip back to the art room. I'm only a couple of minutes late, which is no big deal. As I walk into the room, I lock eyes with Gabby. She excitedly waves at me, and I return the gesture.

Gabby says, "We're working with clay today. Isn't that cool?"

Then Ms. Benedetto walks over with my portfolio and lays it with my backpack. "Here you go, Stella. I kept it safe."

"What's that?" asks Gabby, peeking over at my portfolio.

"It's my artwork for the magnet school application." I look around. "Where is Chris, by the way?"

"Oh, he is still working on his application." Gabby pushes the clay around. "He popped in at the beginning to let Mr. Foster know he was missing today."

At first, I feel nervous. Did I not spend enough time on mine? But then I remember how confident I feel about my application now and try to ignore that thought.

"Can I see your artwork?" Gabby asks. "I won't touch it."

"Sure," I reply as I open it up carefully.

I feel proud when I reveal it. I managed to include many details. Pancho is in the center, but there are also sea turtles, dolphins, sea dragons, and an octopus. I made sure to also draw neat-looking coral and shells, and I snuck a scuba diver into the background. Not to mention, I spent almost two days on it.

"It's beautiful!" Gabby whispers. "It reminds me of the first time I visited the ocean."

I smile. "That's what I was thinking about, too, when I drew it."

"I just love the oceans." Gabby pauses. "It makes me so angry to think that there are people who don't care about them."

"Me too."

Then I look at Gabby and realize something big. I was so afraid of the club changing nearly this whole school year that I didn't think how amazing it could be if it did change! It's been in front of my eyes this whole time. I mean, I even included Gabby in the photo collage for the time capsule about the Sea Musketeers. It would be great to have more members, especially someone who cares like Gabby. I do what I should have done a long time ago.

"Gabby?"

"Yes, Stella?" Her hands are covered in messy clay.

"I'm going to check with the Sea Musketeers about

adding new members." I bite my lip. "I'm sorry it's taken so long. I've been distracted."

"YES!" she exclaims. Then she covers her mouth because she was too loud. She immediately makes a grossed-out expression.

"Ugh, clay doesn't taste good," she replies as she spits.

I giggle. "Good to know."

Chapter Nineteen

"So, Mom, have you received any fun emails about my future?" I ask over my delicious breakfast plate.

It's Saturday morning, and Mom outdid herself for breakfast. She visited a *panadería* at dawn. Then she made us scrambled eggs on top of a freshly baked *bolillo*. I don't know why *bolillos* taste better than regular bread. Maybe because it's crunchy on the outside and super soft on the inside.

Mom shakes her head. "*Nada, mi amor.*" She grabs my empty plate. "And the school said they would let us know some time in April. We still have a couple of weeks left in the month."

I sigh. All I can do is wait. While I'm a bit worried, there is little I can do.

Nick, on the other hand, is having a big Saturday. He's taking his PSATs at school.

"Break a leg," I tell him as he heads out the door.

"No, thank you," he replies with a wink. "One time is enough."

"*Buena suerte, niño,*" Mom says as she hands him a chocolate croissant.

Nick grins. Those are his favorite. "Thanks, Mom."

Mom and I walk Ramona before today's Sea Musketeers meeting. We're hosting it at my house this time. I'm a little nervous because this is the first meeting that Gabby is attending. I tried to bring it up earlier to the group, but we had to skip a meeting because of everyone's schedule and not everyone was there at another meeting. Thankfully, I was finally able to bring it up to the whole group last week, and they seemed to like the idea. They thought she was great at the fundraiser. I hope I'm right.

I'm cleaning my room when I hear the doorbell

ring. Mom answers it, and I immediately recognize who it is by the level of excitement in the voice.

"What a lovely home you have, Ms. Díaz."

"Thank you, Gabby," Mom replies, looking surprised. Then again, Gabby is not like most third graders.

As I walk over, I see Gabby holding a basket of baked goods.

"Wow, did you make those?" I ask. The basket is filled with all types of muffins and cookies, including macarons. I've only seen those at the fancy bakeries.

She grins proudly. "I made them with my parents. We love baking and watching cooking shows together on Friday nights. It's our tradition."

"We have a Friday night tradition, too," I reply. "But we play games, and Mom cooks a special meal."

Mom then adds. "Maybe you can join us sometime, Gabby."

I glance over at Gabby. Maybe that would be nice. Let's see how today goes, though. Then Ramona goes up to Gabby to say hello. She wags her tail, which is a very good sign.

"Do you want to come upstairs and wait in my room until the meeting starts?" I ask.

"Sure!" she replies.

"*Es simpática*," Mom comments that she thinks Gabby is likable.

"Thank you, Ms. Díaz!" replies Gabby from the top step. "My dad is from Mexico. He taught me some Spanish, too."

"*Maravilloso*," Mom adds.

Soon the rest of the group shows up. It feels strange for a little bit, but that quickly goes away. Especially after Gabby hands out baked goods she made for the group.

At the start of the meeting, Logan takes attendance while eating a banana muffin. Then I decide to take the reins. I clear my throat.

"Hi, everyone. So I'm sure you've noticed our special guest today, Gabby."

She squeals a little.

It takes me a second to get the words out of my head, but once I do, it's easy.

"I am excited to welcome her to our group and to start a new era for the Sea Musketeers. Together, we can make a bigger change. More than if we just remained the same."

Stanley replies, "Here, here! I think the more the merrier."

Jenny chimes in. "Plus, as we keep getting busier, it will be nice to know someone can always be doing something for the cause."

Logan grabs his chin. "That's all true, but shouldn't we have an interview and vote to make it official?"

Gabby stands up. "I can do that."

Before we can say anything else, Gabby grabs the toy orca.

"I'm Gabby Torres. I'm in third grade. I love the oceans and all the sea creatures. I used to call them all fishes, but that's wrong because there are all types of animals in the ocean. Mollusks, crustaceans, mammals, just to name a few."

She pauses. "Sorry . . . I ramble sometimes when I'm nervous."

I give her a thumbs-up. She takes a deep breath and then resumes talking more slowly. "And I've wanted to be a Sea Musketeer since I heard about your presentation to the city council in second grade because I want to protect our oceans just like you all. I promise to be a dedicated club member if you let me join. Thank you."

Gabby sits down smiling and lets out a little sigh of relief.

I look around and lock eyes with everyone in the room. It's clear what our decision will be.

"Raise your hand if you want Gabby to be a club member?" I ask.

Everyone raises their hand immediately, and Gabby starts jumping up and down.

"Thank you! Thank you! I have so many ideas, like fundraisers and volunteering." She pulls out a large notebook. "Oh, and some of my friends want to join also."

Logan picks up the orca toy to get the next word in. "That's a good idea. Maybe there could be even more Sea Musketeers clubs."

"Oooh . . . like the Girl Scouts!" exclaims Kristen.

We get to work on how we will add new club members and what the application would look like. I start to grin. With new members like Gabby, I will never have to worry about the Sea Musketeers going away. In fact, this is what the club needed to make sure it continues for a very long time.

Chapter Twenty

We still haven't heard anything about the application toward the end of April. I'm trying to stay optimistic, but it's hard when there's complete radio silence. I feel lost at sea, but at least I'm not alone. Mariel and Chris are in the same boat. I know they are both feeling this way, too. Fortunately, Jenny has a dance recital tonight, which should be a good distraction. I promised her I'd go since she's been such a supportive friend about Chicago Art and Science. Although I wish she would have toured the school at least once before saying no.

It's girls' night because only Mom is going with me to the recital. Nick is hanging out with Erika tonight.

As we walk outside to the car, we see our new neighbors, Amir and Nadia, on their front stoop. They moved into Linda's old place in January. We only met them very briefly then because they just had a baby. Mom says that newborns require a lot of attention.

"Hi, neighbors," Mom says as she waves over to them.

Nadia waves back as Amir brings the stroller down their front steps.

"Hiya!" Amir replies. "Would you finally like to meet Mina, our little one?"

"Of course!" I exclaim. I love babies, and I've never had the chance to meet one so little before.

I lean over and see the sweetest little baby chewing on a pacifier. She's so adorable. As cute as Ramona and Biscuit combined. It's also hard to imagine that I was ever that little. Not only that, when I was her age, we still lived in Mexico! Look how far we've come since then.

"Maybe one day you can watch Mina," Nadia replies. "When she and you are both a little older."

"I'd be happy to!"

I can picture it. I'll be her cool neighbor who is there for her just like Linda was for me. Maybe she can even join the Sea Musketeers one day, and I'll be her mentor!

When we arrive at the recital, Mom saves us two seats as I run backstage to wish Jenny good luck before the performance. With the large crowd, it takes me a while to spot Jenny. I almost don't recognize her. She's wearing her hair in a French braid and wearing a princess costume.

She gives me a hug right away. "Isn't my outfit the coolest?" She's beaming. "We've never worn costumes before in the performances. It's because I'm at a more advanced level."

I reply, "It is!" I mean it, too.

"Kelsey, come over here," exclaims Jenny. She's waving to a girl standing next to the mirror. Jenny whispers, "Kelsey did my hair!"

I wince. Maybe Kelsey and all her dance friends are the real reason Jenny didn't want to apply to the magnet school with me. I start to feel my face turn a little *roja* as she walks over with two girls. But before I can get too upset, Jenny says, "This is Stella. My best, best, bestest friend. This is the one I talk about all the time."

Then I turn more *roja*, but this time it's out of embarrassment. I really should remember not to worry about Jenny.

After I chat and wish them good luck, I run back to the audience and take a seat next to Mom. She is silent and staring at her phone. There are tears in her eyes.

"Oh no, is it bad news?" I whisper.

Then she wipes her eyes and shows me the phone. It's an email from the magnet school.

"Congrats, *niñita*. You did it. You'll be attending the Chicago Art and Science school next fall."

I hug Mom as the lights go out in the auditorium.

Sitting in the dark, I watch mesmerized as Jenny moves on the illuminated stage. I can see fully how much the hard work and time have paid off with Jenny's dancing. She soars in the air like a professional, and I can see how much she puts her heart into it. I realize then that staying at this dance school is the best thing for Jenny, just like attending the magnet school is for me. As long as Jenny and I are there for each other, cheering each other on from the sidelines, our friendship will be A-OK.

Chapter
Twenty-One

I feel excited and nervous as I get ready in front of the mirror.

It's finally here, graduation day.

Jessica and I are also going to reveal the time capsule project to our class for the first time. It feels like a shame to bury it so soon in a capsule, because we've just received it fresh from the printers, too. We scanned all the contributions like Ms. Benedetto taught me and assembled it together in the computer like a photo book. Our project almost ended up being like a mini yearbook, but more special. While a yearbook shares a little picture of you, your class, and big things that happen throughout the year, our time capsule shares all our personal memories and even hopes for the future. It's filled with different stuff, too. Like Isabel, who wrote a letter to her future self, while Ben included a collage of his favorite internet memes. Jessica even wrote a poem about fifth grade. I'm still amazed that for someone who can be mean with her words when she is speaking, Jessica uses words beautifully when she writes. I hope my class likes how it turned out.

While I get ready, I rip the tag off my new floral dress. I smooth it out after I put it on. Then I take a breath and pull off my headband. Mom bought me a special starfish bobby pin for today. I stare in the mirror as I part my curls off to the side of my face. Then I clip one side with the starfish pin. I pause and evaluate. I look different with my hair this way, but that's not a bad thing. Maybe I can wear my hair like this sometimes in middle school and use my headband the rest of the time. Nothing wrong with changing things up once in a while.

"*¿Estás lista?*" Mom asks, leaning into my room.

I turn around. "I think so. You like it?" I point to my hair.

She replies, "*Mi bebé* looks *hermosa*. Like a young lady!"

I hug her tight.

"I'm still the same Stella," I reply, squeezing her. While I'm excited about middle school, I feel less in a rush to skip ahead. I think I'll try to enjoy what's happening day to day more.

Nick comes in wearing a suit.

"Did I interrupt a hugging party?" he asks.

I run over to him and hug him. "Nope. You're invited, Mr. Fourteen Hundred."

Instead of his typical groan, he just hugs me back.

Nick did well on his PSATs. All that studying paid off, because he earned a fourteen hundred out of fifteen hundred and twenty. This is how he earned the new nickname. Now that summer is approaching, we're starting to plan tours at some universities in Chicago.

After breakfast, we drive over to my school for the graduation. They're holding it on the field for an outdoor assembly, on a stage outside with signs that say CONGRATULATIONS FIFTH GRADERS and HAPPY GRADUATION. There isn't assigned seating, so we find seats next to Jenny and her mom.

Jenny's mom says, "We've been holding them for you all."

"Thank you," replies Mom.

I see her give Jenny's mom a little hand squeeze. Mom and Jenny's mom are both single parents. They work so hard to provide for us, and I know they are proud of how far Jenny and I have come.

I search around the field. I wave at Stanley and his parents. Then Chris with his family. They are at the end of a row so his dad can sit comfortably in his wheelchair. I even spy Jessica and give her a thumbs-up. Isabel is sitting in front of us and waves before turning back around.

The crowd grows quiet when Mrs. Hsu, our principal, stands up in front of the lectern.

"Today is a special day," Mrs. Hsu announces. "Your graduation day. I'm so proud of all your accomplishments and excited to see what you will do in the future. To begin, I'd like to recognize a few of our students who made it into special programs next year."

She reads from a piece of paper on the lectern. "Would Christopher Pollard and Estrella Díaz please stand up?"

As I rise, I feel excited. I think I know what she is going to say.

"This is the first year we've had two graduates be accepted into the Chicago Art and Science Magnet School. Let's give these two an applause."

I feel a little overwhelmed as everyone claps. I look over at Jenny, who makes whooping sounds. I laugh a little. I wish she were going to the same school as me, but I also know she's not going anywhere either. She will always be my BFF. Then I glance over at Chris, who waves. I'm so glad he and Mariel made it into the school, too. With the two of them, my new middle school will be less scary.

Mrs. Hsu continues the ceremony by recognizing other students and their accomplishments. To my surprise, Ben made perfect attendance. He stands up and cheers when his name is announced. Then we begin the ceremony. Each teacher hands a diploma to their students on the stage. When it's time to receive my diploma, Mrs. Chen gives me a pat on the back. I unravel it and see a little Post-it note in her handwriting.

Always remember, you have within you the strength, the patience, and the passion to reach for the stars to change the world.

I smile.

It's true. I'm a starfish because, like Mom said, I'm stronger than I realize. I also think I may be a dolphin, too, because they are smart and friendly. And a betta fish because they can put up a fight. But like Nick said, the world can be whatever sea creatures I want it to be. And so can I.

Chapter Twenty-Two

"Do you really like our class time cap-sule?" I ask, showing off the project to my class. Jessica and I already presented to the school during the assembly, but the class wanted a closer look. They are huddled around Jessica and me as we flip through the pages.

"Oh, love it!" shouts Isabel. "It looks like a magazine!"

"That was Jessica's idea," I reply as Jessica smiles.

"It looks awesome," adds Stanley.

"I can send you the file by email if you like, Stanley," Jessica says as she turns *roja*.

"Sure!" Stanley replies while carefully studying the different pages.

I laugh a little. Jessica is not so bad, I've realized. While I don't necessarily want to see her every day, it wouldn't be the end of the world if I did. It also wouldn't be awful if it turns out that she and Stanley like each other. Although she needs to say something to Stanley because he's a bit clueless, I think.

Mrs. Chen walks over. "Are you ready to put it into the capsule?"

We nod. I've taken every picture I can of it, but now it's time to let it go. Just think, the next time someone sees it, it will be twenty-five years from now. I'll be in my thirties. Gasp, that sounds so old.

I stand by Mom and Nick. We watch with the rest of the crowd as they add our contribution into the time capsule container. It's in a waterproof metal box and looks indestructible. After they lock the box, they bury it deep in the ground with a small digger. That way it's not affected by snow and ice. Who knew it would be this complicated? Last, they place a small plaque on the surface so people know where to find it in the future.

Before we leave, I say to my friends, "See you at my house for the party!"

Mom asks, "Are you ready to go?" She extends her hand out for me to grab.

"I think so," I reply, squeezing it.

Nick, Mom, and I slowly walk back to the car.

"Who wants Oberweis?" asks Nick, heading to the driver's seat.

"*Niño*, we have the graduation party at home in an hour. Linda is meeting us there with the cake, too." Mom laughs.

My mouth waters at the thought of another one of Linda's delicious cakes. Linda has visited us so often it's like she's never left our neighborhood.

"Who says we can't do both?" Nick replies, shrugging.

"Yes, *por favor*!" I reply with pleading eyes.

With one look, Mom is convinced and agrees to

make an Oberweis pit stop. When the car starts, Mom turns up her salsa music. We all, even Nick, shimmy along to the beat. As I sway along in the car seat, I feel courageous. Maybe I'll even try a new flavor or topping at Oberweis. I'm off to a new adventure in my life, and a new flavor may be necessary.

As we drive away, I look at Arlington Heights Elementary School for one last time.

It looks smaller than when I first saw it. Elementary

school hasn't always been easy, but I'm going to miss it. That's part of life, I think. Nothing is perfect, and most things eventually change. But some things, like true friendship and family, remain the same. And I, Stella Díaz, have my whole future in front of me.

Acknowledgments

Can you believe it, a fifth Stella Díaz book? My, has she changed and grown up throughout the books. Just like in Stella's life, there have been people over the years who have made a difference in my world. They have all made it possible for me to write this series.

First, I have to thank the readers. I appreciate all the fans making it possible to write more Stella books than I could have imagined. I had the first idea for Stella, a girl with curly hair who loves aquariums, in 2013. By the time this book publishes in 2023, it will have been ten years of having the delightful Stella in my life. I've been cheering her on as much as you have along the way. While this may be the end of the Stella series for a while, I hope her adventures continue in new ways in the future. I hope all of you have kindness toward one another and toward our beautiful planet. Always remember, together we accomplish bigger things than we ever could have done alone.

Second, I must thank my family and friends who have inspired the different characters and story lines. Some of your names are the same and some of them are different, but all of you are special to me. I care for you all deeply.

Next, I must thank my beta readers, Mary, Kyle, and Mom. Thank you for taking the time to read each draft and for your endless encouragement. Writing a book is so much fun, but at times, it's also intimidating and frustrating. You three made it possible for me to finish each book without pulling out all my hair or, even worse, giving up.

Finally, I'd also like to thank the people involved in the creation of this book. Thank you to my agent Linda Pratt and my amazing editor Connie Hsu. Connie, you believed in my early draft in 2014. I'm delighted that we have been able to work together on this journey and excited about new books in the future. A huge thank-you to Kristie Radwilowicz, Veronica Mang, and Elizabeth Holden Clark for their wonderful work on the design of the book. Thank you to everyone at Roaring Brook and Macmillan Children's, including Jennifer Besser, Allison Verost, Jen Edwards, Avia Perez, John Nora, Jordin Streeter, and Nicolás Ore-Giron. Last, thank you to the marketing and publicity teams at Macmillan, especially Mary Van Akin, Tatiana Merced-Zarou, and Cynthia Lliguichuzhca, for championing this book and getting it into the hands of educators and librarians.

To all of you, I send an ocean-size hug and a stellar high five.

Resources

Plant a Billion Trees

nature.org/en-us/get-involved/how-to-help/plant-a
-billion/

Billion Oyster Project

billionoysterproject.org/

National Ocean Science (NOAA)

oceanservice.noaa.gov/kids/

**National Geographic:
How to Save the Planet**

natgeokids.com/uk/discover/science/nature/how
-to-save-the-planet/

Make Your Own Time Capsule

learninglab.si.edu/news/make-your-own-time
-capsule

Tips for Kids Interested in Fundraising

fundraisingexpert.com/fundraising-ideas-kids/